# THE UNTEACHABLES

## ALSO BY GORDON KORMAN

# THE
# UNTEACHABLES

## GORDON KORMAN

**BALZER + BRAY**
*An Imprint of* HarperCollins*Publishers*

Balzer + Bray is an imprint of HarperCollins Publishers.

The Unteachables
Copyright © 2019 by Gordon Korman
All rights reserved. Printed in the United States of America.
No part of this book may be used or reproduced in any manner whatsoever without
written permission except in the case of brief quotations embodied in critical articles
and reviews. For information address HarperCollins Children's Books, a division of
HarperCollins Publishers, 195 Broadway, New York, NY 10007.
www.harpercollinschildrens.com

Library of Congress Control Number: 2018938414
ISBN 978-0-06-256388-0 (trade bdg.)
ISBN 978-0-06-256389-7 (lib. bdg.)

Typography by Erin Fitzsimmons
18  19  20  21  22    CG/LSCH    10 9 8 7 6 5 4 3 2 1

First Edition

*For all the teachers who soldier on*

# One

## Kiana Roubini

I t's no fun riding to school with Stepmonster—not with Chauncey screaming his lungs out in the back seat.

Don't get me wrong. I'd cry too if I'd just figured out that Stepmonster is my mother. But at seven months old, I don't think he's processed that yet. He just cries. He cries when he's hungry; he cries when he's full; he cries when he's tired; he cries when he wakes up after a long nap. Basically, any day that ends in a *y*, Chauncey cries.

There also seems to be a connection between his volume control and the gas pedal of the SUV. The louder he howls, the faster Stepmonster drives.

"Who's a happy baby?" she coos over her shoulder into the back seat, where the rear-facing car seat is anchored. "Who's a happy big boy?"

"Not Chauncey, that's for sure," I tell her. "Hey— school zone. You better slow down."

She speeds up. "Motion is soothing to a baby."

Maybe so. But as we slalom up the driveway, swerving around parked parents dropping off their kids, and screech to a halt by the entrance, it turns out to be one motion too many. Chauncey throws up his breakfast. Suddenly, there's cereal on the ceiling and dripping down the windows. That's another thing about Chauncey. His stomach is a food expander. It goes in a teaspoon and comes out five gallons.

"Get out of the car!" Stepmonster orders frantically.

"You have to come in with me," I protest. "They won't let me register without an adult."

She looks frazzled, and I guess I don't blame her. That much baby puke must be hard to face. "I'll run home, change him, and wipe down the car. Wait for me. Ten minutes—fifteen at the most."

What can I do? I haul my backpack out of the SUV, and she zooms off around the circular drive. I don't even have the chance to make my usual Parmesan cheese joke—that's what it smells like when Chauncey barfs. When I first came from California to stay with Dad and Stepmonster, I thought they ate a lot of Italian food. That was a disappointment—one of many.

So there I am in front of Greenwich Middle School, watching swarms of kids arriving for the first day of classes. A few of them glance in my direction, but not many. New girl; who cares? Actually, the new girl doesn't much care either. I'm a short-timer—I'm only in Greenwich for a couple of months while Mom is off in Utah shooting a movie. She's not a star or anything like that, but this could be her big break. After years of paying the bills with bit parts in sitcoms and TV commercials, she finally landed an independent film. Well, no way could I go with her for eight weeks—not that I was invited.

Eventually, a bell rings and the crowd melts into the school. No Stepmonster. I'm officially late, which isn't the best way to start my career in Greenwich. But short-timers don't stress over things like that.

3

Long before it could come back to haunt me on a report card, I'll be ancient history.

I check on my phone. It's been twenty minutes since "ten minutes—fifteen at the most." That's SST—Stepmonster Standard Time. I try calling, but she doesn't pick up. Maybe that means she's on her way and will be here any second.

But a lot of seconds tick by. No barf-encrusted SUV.

With a sigh, I sit myself down on the bench at student drop-off and prop my backpack up on the armrest beside me. Stepmonster—her real name is Louise—isn't all that monstrous when you think about it. She's way less out of touch than Dad, which might be because she's closer to my age than his. She isn't exactly thrilled with the idea of having an eighth grader dropped in her lap right when she's getting the hang of being a new mom. She's trying to be nice to me—she just isn't succeeding. Like when she strands me in front of a strange school when she's supposed to be here to get me registered.

The roar of an engine jolts me back to myself. For a second I think it must be her. But no—a rusty old pickup truck comes sailing up the roadway, going much faster than even Stepmonster would dare. As it reaches the bend in the circular drive, the front tire climbs the curb, and the pickup is coming right at me. Acting on instinct alone, I hurl myself over the back of the bench and out of the way.

The truck misses the bench by about a centimeter. The side mirror knocks my book bag off the armrest, sending it airborne. The contents—binders, papers, pencil case, gym shorts, sneakers, lunch—are scattered to the four winds, raining down on the pavement.

The pickup screeches to a halt. The driver jumps out and starts rushing after my fluttering stuff. As he runs, papers fly out of his shirt pocket, and he's chasing his own things, not just mine.

I join the hunt, and that's when I get my first look at the guy. He's a kid—like, around my age! "Why are you driving?" I gasp, still in shock from the near miss.

"I have a license," he replies, like it's the most normal thing in the world.

"No way!" I shoot back. "You're no older than I am!"

"I'm fourteen." He digs around in his front pocket and pulls out a laminated card. It's got a picture of his stupid face over the name Parker Elias. At the top it says: PROVISIONAL LICENSE.

"Provisional?" I ask.

"I'm allowed to drive for the family business," he explains.

"Which is what—a funeral parlor? You almost killed me."

"Our farm," he replies. "I take produce to the market. Plus, I take my grams to the senior center. She's super old and doesn't drive anymore."

I've never met a farmer before. There aren't a lot of them in LA. I knew Greenwich was kind of the boonies, but I never expected to be going to school with Old MacDonald.

He hands me my book bag with my stuff crammed in every which way. There's a gaping hole where the mirror blasted through the vinyl.

"I'm running late," he stammers. "Sorry about the backpack." He jumps in the pickup, wheels it into a parking space, and races into the building, studiously avoiding my glare.

Still no sign of Stepmonster on the horizon. I call again. Straight to voice mail.

I decide to tackle the school on my own. Maybe I can get a head start filling out forms or something.

The office is a madhouse. It's packed with kids who a) lost their schedules, b) don't understand their schedules, or c) are trying to get their schedules changed. When I tell the harassed secretary that I'm waiting for my parent and/or guardian so I can register, she just points to a chair and ignores me.

Even though I have nothing against Greenwich Middle School, I decide to hate it. Who can blame me? It's mostly Chauncey's fault, but let's not forget Parker McFarmer and his provisional license.

My phone pings. A text from Stepmonster: *Taking Chauncey to pediatrician. Do your best without me. Will get there ASAP.*

The secretary comes out from behind the counter and stands before me, frowning. "We don't use our phones in school. You'll have to turn that off and leave it in your locker."

"I don't have a locker," I tell her. "I just moved here. I have no idea where I'm supposed to be."

She plucks a paper from the sheaf sticking out of the hole in my backpack. "It's right here on your schedule."

"Schedule?" Where would I get a schedule? I don't even officially go to school here yet.

"You're supposed to be in room 117." She rattles off a complicated series of directions. "Now, off you go."

And off I go. I'm so frazzled that I'm halfway down the main hall before I glance at the paper that's supposed to be a schedule. It's a schedule, all right—just not mine.

At the top, it says: ELIAS, PARKER. GRADE: 8.

This is Parker McFarmer's schedule! It must have gotten mixed up with my papers when we were gathering up all my stuff.

I take three steps back in the direction of the office and freeze. I don't want to face that secretary again. There's no way she's going to register me without Stepmonster. And if there's a backlog at the pediatrician's, I'm going to be sitting in that dumb chair all day. No, thanks.

I weigh my options. It's only a fifteen-minute walk home. But home isn't really home, and I don't want to be there any more than I want to be here. If I went to all the trouble of waking up and getting ready for school, then school is where I might as well be.

My eyes return to Parker's schedule. Room 117. Okay, it's not *my* class, but it's *a* class. And really, who cares? It's not like I'm going to learn anything in the next two months—at least nothing I can't pick up when I get back to civilization. I'm a pretty good student. And when Stepmonster finally gets here, they can page me and send me to the right place—not that I'll learn anything there either. I've already learned the one lesson Greenwich Middle School has to teach me: fourteen-year-olds shouldn't drive.

That's when I learn lesson number two: this place is a maze. My school in LA is all outdoors—you step out of class and you're in glorious sunshine. You know where you're going next because you can see it across the quad. And the numbers make sense. Here, 109 is next to 111, but the room next to that is labeled STORAGE CLOSET E61-B2. Go figure.

I ask a couple of kids, who actually try to tell me that there's no such room as 117.

"There has to be," I tell the second guy. "I'm in it." I show him the schedule, careful to cover the name with my thumb.

"Wait." His brow furrows. "What's"—he points to the class description—"SCS-8?"

I blink. Instead of a normal schedule, where you go to a different class every period, this says Parker stays in room 117 all day. Not only that, but under SUB-JECT, it repeats the code SCS-8 for every hour except LUNCH at 12:08.

"Oh, here it is." I skip to the bottom, where there's a key explaining what the codes mean. "SCS-8—Self-Contained Special Eighth-Grade Class."

He stares at me. "The *Unteachables*?"

"Unteachables?" I echo.

He reddens. "You know, like the Untouchables.

Only—uh"—babbling now—"these kids aren't untouchable. They're—well—unteachable. Bye!" He rushes off down the hall.

And I just know. I could read it in his face, but I didn't even need that much information. Where would you stick a guy who could annihilate a backpack with a half-ton pickup truck? The Unteachables are the dummy class. We have a couple of groups like that in my middle school in California too. We call them the Disoriented Express, but it's the same thing. Probably every school has that.

I almost march back to the office to complain when I remember I've got nothing to complain about. Nobody put *me* in the Unteachables—just Parker. From what I've seen, he's in the right place.

I picture myself, sitting in the office all day, waiting for Stepmonster to arrive. *If* she arrives. Chauncey's health scares—which happen roughly every eight minutes—stress her out to the point where she can't focus on anything else. To quote Dad, "Jeez, Louise." He really says that—an example of the sense of humor of the non-California branch of my family.

So I go to room 117—turns out, it's in the far corner of the school, over by the metal shop, the home and careers room, and the custodian's office. You have to walk past the gym, and the whole hallway smells like old sweat socks mixed with a faint barbecue scent. It's only temporary, I remind myself. And since my whole time in Greenwich is temporary anyway, it's more like temporary squared.

Besides—dummy class, Disoriented Express, Unteachables—so what? Okay, maybe they're not academic superstars, but they're just kids, no different from anybody else. Even Parker—he's a menace to society behind the wheel of that truck, but besides that he's a normal eighth grader, like the rest of us.

Seriously, how unteachable can these Unteachables be?

I push open the door and walk into room 117.

A plume of smoke is pouring out the single open window. It's coming from the fire roaring in the wastebasket in the center of the room. A handful of kids are gathered around it, toasting marshmallows skewered on the end of number two pencils. Parker is one of them, his own marshmallow blackened like a charcoal briquette.

An annoyed voice barks, "Hey, shut the door! You want to set off the smoke detector in the hall?"

Oh my God, I'm with the Unteachables.

# Two

## Mr. Kermit

The first day of school.

I remember the excitement. New students to teach. New minds to fill with knowledge. New futures to shape.

The key word is *remember.* That was thirty years ago. I was so young—not much older than the kids, really. Being a teacher was more than a job. It was a calling, a mission. True, mission: impossible, but I didn't know that back then. I wanted to be Teacher of the Year. I actually achieved that goal.

That was when the trouble started.

Anyway, I don't get excited by the first day anymore. The things that still get my fifty-five-year-old motor running are the smaller pleasures: the last tick of the clock before the three-thirty bell sounds; waking up in the morning and realizing it's Saturday; the glorious voice of the weather forecaster: *Due to the snowstorm, all schools are closed down . . .*

And the most beautiful word of all: *retirement.* The first day of school means it's only ten months away. My younger self never could have imagined I'd turn into the kind of teacher who'd be crunching numbers, manipulating formulas, and counting the nanoseconds until I can kiss the classroom and everybody in it goodbye. Yet here I am.

I sip from my super-large coffee mug. The other teachers call it the Toilet Bowl when they think I'm not listening. They gripe that I owe extra money to the faculty coffee fund because I drink more than my fair share. Tough. The students are bad enough, but the dunderheads who teach them are even worse. Colleagues—they don't know the meaning of the word. A fat lot of support they ever offered me when it was all going wrong.

"Mr. Kermit."

Dr. Thaddeus is standing over me in the faculty room, his three-thousand-dollar suit tailored just so. Superintendent. Major dictator. A legend in his own mind.

Christina Vargas, the principal, is with him. "Nice to see you, Zachary. How was your summer?"

"Hot," I tell her, but she keeps on smiling. She's one of the good ones, which puts me on my guard. Thaddeus uses her to do his dirty work. Something is coming. I can smell it.

"There's been a change in the schedule," the super-intendent announces. "Christina will fill you in on the details."

"As you know, Mary Angeletto has left the district," the principal says. "So we're moving you into her spot with the Self-Contained Special Eighth-Grade Class."

I stare at her. "You mean the *Unteachables*?"

Dr. Thaddeus bristles. "We don't use that term."

"Every teacher in this building knows what they are," I fire back. "They're the kids you've given up on. They had their chance in sixth and seventh grade, and now you're just warehousing them until they can be the high school's problem."

"They're a challenging group," Christina concedes.

"Which is why we've chosen a teacher with a great deal of experience."

"Of course," the superintendent goes on pleasantly, "if you don't feel you're *up* to the job—"

Light dawns. So *that's* what this is really about. Thaddeus figured out that I qualify for early retirement after this year. He doesn't want the school district on the hook supporting me forever. The Kermit men live till ninety-five, minimum. My grandfather, at 106, is still president of the shuffleboard club at Shady Pines. That's why they're giving me the Unteachables. They aren't interested in my experience. They want my resignation.

I look the superintendent right in his snake eyes. "You're just trying to make me quit before I qualify for early retirement."

His response is all innocence. "You're up for retirement already? I think of you as so young. It still seems quite recent—that horrible Terranova incident. The media attention. The public outcry. The scandal."

Well, there it is. Jake Terranova. Thaddeus is never going to forgive and forget, even though it wasn't my fault. Or maybe it was. They were my students, after all, and it happened on my watch.

What a hypocrite. Thaddeus wasn't superintendent

then. He had Christina's job—principal. And did he ever take the credit when a class at his school scored number one in the country on the National Aptitude Test. He squeezed every ounce of glory out of that—interviews, profiles in magazines. When there was traffic in the driveway, you could bet it was because of a TV station mobile unit on its way to interview the high-exalted lord of all principals.

Until the truth came out. A kid named Jake Terranova had gotten hold of the test and charged his classmates ten bucks a pop for a copy of it. That's why they aced it—they were cheating. And when the whole thing blew up, was Thaddeus there to take the heat the way he'd taken the acclaim? Not on your life. The teacher was to blame. That's who I've been ever since. The guy who . . . The teacher whose class gave the entire Greenwich School District a black eye.

Officially, life went on after that. No one revoked my teaching certificate or docked my pay or kicked me out of the union. But everything was different. When I stepped into the faculty room, people stopped talking. Colleagues wouldn't look me in the eye. Administration kept changing my department. One year it was English, then math, French, social studies, even phys ed—me with my two left feet.

I went into a blue funk. Okay, that wasn't the school's fault, but it began to affect my personal life. My engagement to Fiona Bertelsman fell apart. That was on me. I was lost in my own misery.

Worst of all, the one thing that was most important to me—teaching—became a bad joke. The students didn't want to learn? Fine. I didn't particularly want to teach them. All I needed to do for my paycheck was show up.

Until next June, when early retirement would carry me away from all of this.

And now Thaddeus thinks he can make me throw that away too, just to avoid a year with the Unteachables. Obviously, the superintendent doesn't have the faintest idea who he's messing with. I would happily go into room 117 with a pack of angry wildcats before I'd give him the satisfaction of forcing me out.

I look from the superintendent to the principal and back to the superintendent again. "I enjoy a good challenge." I pick up the Toilet Bowl and walk out of there, careful to keep the big mug steady. Can't risk spilling coffee all over myself. It would spoil the dramatic exit.

Three decades in this school, and never once have I set foot inside room 117. I know where it is, though, from the stint in phys ed. Somebody has to be in the remotest classroom of the entire building, but I decide to be offended by it. It's just another part of the conspiracy to force me out.

Well, it won't work. After all, how bad can these Unteachables really be? Behavior issues, learning problems, juvenile delinquents? Does Thaddeus honestly think I've never crossed paths with students like that throughout thirty years in the classroom? Bad attitudes? The kid hasn't been born with an attitude that's half as bad as mine at this point. Face it, the Unteachables can only hurt you if you try to teach them. I gave up on teaching anybody anything decades ago. Since then, my relationship with my classes has been one of uncomfortable roommates. We don't much like each other, but everybody knows that if we just hold our noses and keep our mouths shut, we'll eventually get what we want. For me, that means early retirement. For the SCS-8 students, it means being promoted to ninth grade.

That part's a slam dunk, because surely the middle school is dying to get rid of them. What would they have to do to get held back—burn the whole place to the ground?

I walk into my new classroom.

A roaring fire in a wastebasket. Smoke pouring through the open windows. Kids toasting marshmallows on the end of pencils. Pencils catching fire. One pyromaniac-in-training seeing if he can get his eraser to burn. An escapee standing outside in the bushes, gazing in, eyes wide with fear. A boy draped over a desk, fast asleep, oblivious to it all.

Most kids would scramble to look innocent and be sitting up straight with their arms folded in front of them once the teacher puts in an appearance. Not this crew. If I came in with a platoon of ski marine paratroopers, it wouldn't make any more of an impression.

I stroll over to the flaming wastebasket and empty the giant cup of coffee onto the bonfire, which goes out with a sizzle. Silence falls in room 117.

"Good morning," I announce, surveying the room. "I'm your teacher, Mr. Kermit."

Only ten months until June.

# Three

## Parker Elias

I love the sound the pickup truck makes when the motor roars to life. It's even cooler now, with that little muffler problem, but that'll only last until Mom and Dad save up the money to get it fixed. Even without the extra noise, though, it's still awesome.

I look down at the start button:

NEEGIN
RATTS/POTS

That's what I saw the first time, anyway. Now I know that it really says:

ENGINE
START/STOP

That's what reading is for me. I *see* all the letters, but they're kind of a mishmash. Like my class at school, which is SCS-8, although it looks like SS8-C or S8-SC or even C-S8S. It messes me up at first a little until I figure out where I have to go, and then it doesn't matter what order the letters and numbers are in.

The pickup jounces over the packed dirt of the driveway before bumping onto the paved road where our property ends. Our farm is right outside town, so I haven't gone very far when a police car pulls up beside me. The cop gives me a thorough once-over with his eyes. I'm used to it. I'm kind of small for my age, so I look like a twelve-year-old out for a joyride. I thought that new girl's eyes would pop out of her head when I jumped down from the pickup on the first day of school. Or maybe that's the expression she gives everybody who knocks her book bag halfway to the moon.

Let's set the record straight: I'm fourteen. They

don't let you drive any younger than that no matter what your special situation is.

It's okay, though. The police around here all know me. The cop rolls down his window and peers into the flatbed of the pickup, taking note of several bushel baskets of fresh tomatoes.

"You're just taking those over to the farmers' market, right, Parker?" he calls.

"Right, Officer."

"And straight to school after that?"

I shake my head. "First I have to pick up Grams."

The cop frowns. "Grams?"

"My grandmother," I explain. "I have to take her to the senior center. Then school."

That's why I have a driver's license in eighth grade. It's a *provisional* license—although, to me, it usually looks more like RIVALSNOOPI ICELENS. I'm allowed to drive the pickup, so long as it's for farm business or for Grams, who's pretty old and sometimes kind of confused, no offense. My folks both work crazy hours on the farm, so I'm the only one who's free to pick her up at her apartment and take her to the center, where she hangs out all day. Then I drive to school, and after school, I pick her up and take her back to our house for dinner. She doesn't live with us, though. She refuses to give up her own place. "My independence," she calls it.

The law says I can do all this because running a farm is considered a "hardship." That's pretty stupid because we actually prefer living outside the city and having tons of open space when everybody else is stuck on a little postage stamp of grass. Plus, we don't have live-stock, so we don't have to do any of the really gross farm things, like sticking your arm up the butt of a sick cow. (I've only seen that on TV, but—hard pass.)

I drop off the tomatoes at the market, watching the clock impatiently while Mr. Sardo weighs everything to the millionth of an ounce. Then straight to Grams. She's waiting for me in the lobby of her apartment building, but she's wearing a winter coat, and it's like eighty degrees out. So I have to park and we go upstairs to put away the coat, and by the time I return from the closet, she's in the kitchen, warming up left-over meatloaf for me.

"But Grams, I'm going to be late for school."

"Breakfast is the most important meal of the day, kiddo."

I used to like it when she called me kiddo—but now I'm pretty sure it's because she can't remember my name. It bums me out. To be fair, she called me kiddo before she forgot my name too. The difference is now it's the *only* thing she calls me.

"I already *had* breakfast," I tell her.

"You want mashed potatoes with that?" she asks. "It won't take long."

"No, thanks. This is fine."

Obviously, I eat the meatloaf. It's actually pretty good. Grams can still cook, even though she's forgotten most other things. She's been knitting me a sweater for the past three years that she can't seem to finish. I've gotten a lot bigger in that time, but it's okay, because so has the sweater. It's draped over the back of the couch, a mass of dropped stitches, hanging strands, and random colors. It looks like a giant psychedelic wool amoeba.

I gulp down the food as fast as I can, but it still throws off the schedule. By the time I drop Grams at the senior center, I can already hear the bell ringing at school. With my grandmother, there's always something to slow you down—if isn't meatloaf, then she's buttoned her blouse wrong, or she's wearing slippers instead of shoes, or she's waiting for Grandpa to come home, even though he died a long time ago. I'm used to being late—Grams is worth it. But it's my fourth time already, and it's only the first week of school.

I barrel around the streets, busting the speed limit by

a lot, and blowing at least one stop sign. I screech into the school parking lot, leaving a small mark on the side of Mr. Sarcassian's BMW. Not good. Carefully, I back out and find another spot, this one on the opposite side of the lot. I pull my trusty can of scratch guard out of the glove compartment and rub the evidence off my front bumper. Then I work on the Beemer a little. Not perfect, but it should keep Mr. S. from noticing the damage long enough for him to have absolutely no idea where it might have come from.

This is usually the part where my day starts to go downhill. I love getting to school—the driving and all that. But once I'm here—not so much. There's no problem with the building, and the teachers are okay, I guess. It just happens to be a place where I'm bad at everything that's considered important.

It's a long walk to room 117. I take it slow, because who wants to rush to somewhere you hate? I'm already late, though, so I open the door and walk inside.

Before I know it, my feet slide out from under me, and *wham!* I'm flat on my back on the floor.

It gets a big laugh and scattered applause from the six kids who are already there. The only person who doesn't react is our teacher, Mr. Kermit. He never lifts his face from the *New York Times* crossword puzzle, except occasionally to take a sip from a humongous coffee cup. And that's not just today. He's like that all the time. Yesterday, when Barnstorm chucked one of his crutches and shattered the globe, the teacher didn't so much as flinch, not even when the Horn of Africa bounced off the side of his head. You could probably set off an atomic bomb on his desk, and he'd never notice.

I scramble up. But when I turn back to the doorway to see what tripped me, I go down again, on my face this time. I can smell the floor, and taste it a little. There's butter all over it!

"Who greased the floor?" I howl.

The kids laugh louder—enough to penetrate the cone of silence and capture Mr. Kermit's attention. He glances up, sees me flopping like a fish out of water, and quickly goes back to his puzzle. If he's not the worst teacher in the world, he's definitely bottom five.

Most embarrassing of all, Kiana has to rescue me— she's the girl whose backpack I hit with the truck. She hauls me far enough from the buttered area that I can stand upright again. My shoes are still a little slippery, but at least I can walk to my desk.

Kiana turns to the rest of the class. "Who did that?"

Rahim, who's fast asleep, lifts his head off the desk and looks around like a deer in headlights. "Did what?"

"Let it go," I murmur, red-faced.

"Why should you?" she demands. "Somebody buttered the doorway. Mr. Kermit's not going to stand for that."

An absentminded "Mmmm" comes from the direction of the teacher's desk.

"Shhh!" I drag my broken body into my chair. Who's the mystery prankster who almost put me in intensive care? Plenty of possibilities in this class. Barnstorm, the injured sports star. He gets away with everything— at least he did until they put him in SCS-8. Aldo, the jerk who flies off the handle every time the wind blows. Elaine—I sneak a look over my shoulder at the scariest girl in the eighth grade. Oh, please don't let it be her. Elaine rhymes with pain.

I'll probably never find out who buttered the floor. If it was Elaine, I don't want to.

When I glance up, Mr. Kermit is standing in front of me. At first I'm flattered that he's come over to make sure I don't have a concussion. But no. He places a worksheet on my desk and wordlessly returns to his crossword puzzle.

That's what we do in the Special Self-Contained Eighth-Grade Class. At the beginning of each period, Mr. Kermit hands us each a worksheet. No one does them.

At least that's how it was at the beginning. There were a lot of paper airplanes sailing around the room for the first few days. I figured Mr. Kermit would get mad, but he never made a peep about them. So the airplanes stopped. What was the point of making them if you couldn't get a rise out of the teacher? Eventually, it got so boring that the only possible thing to do was the worksheet.

It's kind of hard for me, though, because the letters get all jumbled up. Even if it's math, they never just ask what's five plus three. They have to make it into a story about five brown rabbits and three white rabbits having a rabbit cotillion. That's where I get lost. *Cotillion* looks like *licit loon* to me.

I'm hunched over my paper, trying to make heads or tails of what seems to be unbreakable code, when, at the desk beside me, Kiana sets down her pen and peers at my paper, which is as untouched as the minute I got it.

"You haven't started yet?" she hisses.

"Sure I have," I reply defensively.

She isn't sold. "What question are you on?"

"One," I shoot back. "I'm taking it slow, okay?" I return to work, staring at the letters, willing them to arrange themselves into a form that makes sense to me.

I guess I look like a scientist peering into a microscope, because she blurts, "You can't read!"

"Yes I can!" I say defensively. "I'm just—pacing myself."

She reaches over and plants a finger on question one. "What does that say?"

"There's no talking in class," I tell her. "You want to get us in trouble?"

Mr. Kermit takes a long, loud slurp of his giant coffee.

"Read it!" she orders.

And I don't. It's not that I can't. But it would take time. "I don't feel like it," I mumble.

"Parker," she urges, "this is stupid. You can get help with this. You just have to tell the teacher. But nobody can help you if they don't know there's a problem!"

My eyes find Mr. Kermit. His attention never wavers from his crossword puzzle, even though Rahim and Barnstorm are sword fighting with rulers, and Aldo leaves the room altogether. If I have to depend on Mr. Kermit for help, I'm going to be older than he is before I get any.

# Four

## Aldo Braff

The first time I saw Kiana, I knew she was going to be a pain in my neck.

It was the first day of school—the marshmallow roast. She was the new girl, so I was nice. I took a pencil, speared a marshmallow, and made room for her around the fire. Talk about rude! She refused to take it because it was "unsanitary."

That's the last time I try to be a gentleman.

You know those bossy types who think they know everything? That's Kiana. One time I'm in the cafeteria when she comes up to me and tells me to stop kicking the candy machine.

If I'm kicking the candy machine, I'm doing it for a very good reason! Who put her in charge of the world?

She grabs my arm and hauls me away from the machine. "What's wrong?"

"I wanted a Zagnut!" I tell her in fury. "It gave me a Mounds!"

"So?"

Man, she really isn't from around here. At Greenwich Middle School, everybody knows two things about me: 1) when I want something, nothing stands in my way, and 2) I don't like coconut.

I look around. There's dead silence in the cafeteria, but nobody's eyes are on me. They know better than to get between me and a Zagnut bar. All except Kiana. Maybe all Californians are like that. They can't mind their own business.

She asks, "And if you keep on kicking it, will the Zagnut come out?"

"Maybe," I say stubbornly.

She shrugs. "Then go ahead."

But here's the thing: I don't want to kick it anymore. She's ruined it for me!

The worst part is, she's in SCS-8, so I can never get away from her. We spend the whole day in room 117, except for lunch in the cafeteria and phys ed, which is in the gym with a couple of other classes. The only surefire place to avoid her is the boys' room. She hasn't followed me in there. So far.

Our teacher, Mr. Kermit, is probably in his fifties, but he looks about nine hundred. Actually, he looks like he's dead already, hunched over his desk, his eyes half-closed. He never moves a muscle. It's hard to tell if he's even breathing. I'm amazed he isn't swinging from the light fixture, for all the coffee the guy drinks. Mostly, he's working on a really complicated crossword puzzle. He hates my guts—at least I think he does. All the teachers in this dump have it out for me, so why should he be any different?

He's dumb too. He doesn't even realize that we all call him Ribbit. There's this nut job in our class, Mateo Hendrickson—he pointed out that the only Kermit he ever heard of was Kermit the Frog. Turns out Mateo's a fan of the Muppets, not just *Star Trek*,

*Star Wars*, *Harry Potter*, *Halo*, and every comic book ever printed.

Anyway, a nickname was born. Every morning when the teacher walks in, late as usual, we start rib-biting.

*"Ribbit . . . Ribbit . . . Ribbit . . ."*

Mr. Kermit doesn't even notice. Either that or he thinks it's a compliment.

As a teacher, he stinks—not that I've had any good ones. He never gives lessons. In fact, he hardly ever speaks out loud. He just passes around these stupid worksheets all day long. Boring doesn't even begin to describe it.

With a normal teacher, if you don't do the work, you get in trouble. Not Ribbit. He acts like he couldn't care less if we do his worksheets or not.

"I've turned in every assignment and he's never graded a single one or handed it back," Kiana complains. "What's he doing with them?"

"Maybe he's eating them," I suggest. "He's weird enough."

She rolls her eyes at me.

She's annoying, but it's not like the other kids in SCS-8 are any better. There's Parker Elias, who has to be the dumbest person in the whole school. Remember the kid in first grade who, when he got picked to read aloud, everybody else wanted to drink bleach? Well, Parker still reads that way today—one word at a time, at the speed of molasses, sounding out every letter. This is the idiot they give a special driver's license to. No one is safe.

There's Barnstorm Anderson, super jock. Super jerk would be more like it, but I guess he's both. He's an unstoppable running back, an amazing point guard, and a lights-out pitcher, which is why the school gives him an automatic get-out-of-jail-free card. That makes me mad—why should scoring touchdowns mean you get special treatment? But here's the thing: last spring, Barnstorm blew out his knee. He's on crutches now, banned from sports for a whole year, and by that time, he won't be in middle school anymore. So all the teachers have suddenly started to notice that the last time he turned in a homework assignment was never.

That's the kind of person who lands in our class. Like Elaine Ostrover, who sits in the back row. She has to be six foot two and is solid as an oak tree. She hardly ever opens her mouth, but when she does, her voice comes out a low rumble, like a subwoofer.

Kiana asks me about her.

"That's Elaine," I reply. "Rhymes with pain."

She frowns. "Everybody says that—'rhymes with pain.' What does it mean?"

"You don't want to mess with Elaine," I advise her seriously. "Last year she head-butted this kid down the stairs because he was looking at her funny. Wiped out, like, fifteen people. The line outside the nurse's office stretched halfway to the cafeteria. If that's not pain, I don't know what is."

Kiana checks out Elaine's head, which looks like one of those giant statues on that island from the cover of our world geography textbook.

"She has to register her head as a deadly weapon with the FBI," I put in.

Kiana skewers me with a sharp glance, so I say, "Well, not really. But she definitely tore the door off one of the bathroom stalls and used it to crush the laminating machine." I add, "I mean, I wasn't *there*, but everybody knows it."

"You're scared of her," Kiana decides.

"I'm not scared! I can handle Elaine—rhymes with pain." If you don't say the full name, it increases your chances of being the next victim. "I just—don't want to get in trouble for fighting, that's all."

She nods. "Because you're the big expert at not getting in trouble."

By the time I realize that I'm mad at her for saying that, she's on the other side of the room, and the chance to yell at her is lost forever.

Rahim Barclay is supposed to be this amazing artist, although all I've ever seen him do is doodle. I guess his doodles are pretty good, if you're into that kind of thing. He drew one of Ribbit that's a dead ringer for our teacher—the sunken cheeks and dark circles around the eyes. Just the right amount of gray in the thinning hair. Rahim blew one part of it—he drew the coffee mug too big, almost the size of a trash barrel. Maybe that's how he ended up in SCS-8, which isn't exactly for geniuses. It doesn't help that Rahim's stepdad is in a rock band. They practice all night, so Rahim sleeps most of the day.

One day Mateo welcomes me to class with a whole story in this deep, throat-clearing gibberish that sounds a lot like he's trying to spit out a bug he swallowed by mistake.

I don't appreciate being messed with—especially when I'm not even sure *how* I'm being messed with. "What did you say?" I demand.

"It's a Klingon greeting!" Mateo explains cheerfully. "It means, 'May you die well.'"

My eyes widen. "You want me to *die*?"

"The Klingons are a warlike race!" Mateo says quickly. "Dying in battle is an honor. They love that!"

"But I don't! From now on, if you've got anything to say to me, say it in English, not some phony language—"

"Klingon is *not* phony!" Mateo cuts me off, outraged. "It may have started out on *Star Trek*, but it's turned into a legitimate language with a dictionary and an alphabet. There are even regional accents, depending on which part of the Klingon home world you come from. In the south, for example . . ."

He keeps talking—*lecturing*—clueless that my blood is boiling. And the other kids are *laughing*! Like it's a big joke that this little creep is making fun of me!

"What's the matter with you?" I shout at them. "Doesn't anybody have my back?"

Kiana steps forward, struggling to keep a straight face. She reaches for my arm. "Aldo—"

It's the last straw—that this California girl, who isn't even from around here, thinks I'm the entertainment.

A soupy fog swirls around my head, tinged with orange, until I can actually feel the heat from it. I've got to get out of here before I explode, leaving bone fragments and bits of skin all over the walls of room 117.

*"I hate this class!"* I pick up my backpack and hurl it through the open door—just as Mr. Kermit walks into the room. The heavy bag misses his head by about a quarter of an inch. At that point, I'm so mad I don't even care. In my white-hot haze, it would make no difference to me if the backpack knocks the teacher's block off and I get suspended, expelled, and banished from the town. I do notice, through my rage, that Ribbit doesn't flinch—not even when I storm past him, slamming the door behind me hard enough to raise the school off its foundation.

And just like that, I'm alone in the hall, barely sure how I even got there. I slam my fist into a locker. It hurts, but I hope it hurts the locker even more. The locker is attached to the wall, and the wall is part of the school. And it's the school's fault that I'm so mad. I hit it a few more times—with an open hand, because that hurts a bit less. I don't feel better, exactly. It's more like every blow lets off a little more steam, so the pressure inside my head goes down. I'm still ticked off, but I can live with it. I slump against the lockers, breathing hard.

The guidance counselors say I have anger management problems. They don't know what they're talking about. I manage to get angry better than anybody else in the whole school. No problem.

The door of room 115 opens and this lady walks up to me. At first, I think she could be another eighth grader—that's how young she looks. But no, she's definitely an adult. And the way she takes hold of my wrist—gentle but with authority—screams *teacher*. I've never seen her before, so she must be new.

"Come with me." She knocks on the door of SCS-8. "Mr. Kermit?"

I shoulder my backpack and stand behind her. We wait at the door, but there's no answer.

"He's probably in the middle of a puzzle," I offer in a subdued voice.

"Puzzle?" she echoes.

"Like a crossword. Ribbit—uh, Mr. Kermit—is really into them."

She knocks again and then opens the door. It sticks a little, and she has to put her shoulder into it. I guess I slammed it really hard. She leads me inside. Kiana is looking right at me. I feel myself starting to get mad again, but only for a second. It doesn't usually happen twice in a row.

"Mr. Kermit, I'm Emma Fountain," the woman introduces herself. "I have the class next door."

So far this year, not a single thing has gotten a reaction out of Ribbit. That streak ends here. The puzzle forgotten, he rises to his feet really slowly, never taking his eyes off her. They're practically bugging out of his head!

He blurts, "I'd know you anywhere!"

She smiles, which makes her seem even younger. "Mom said to tell you hi. But that's not why I'm here." She indicates me. "Is this your student?"

Mr. Kermit looks blank. It hits me—he doesn't have a clue, even though I nearly took his head off with my backpack ninety seconds ago! My own teacher doesn't know me from Jack the Ripper.

"Of course it's your student!" Kiana pipes up. "It's Aldo!"

"Well, he's making a lot of noise in the hall," Miss Fountain announces. "That's not being a bucket-filler."

Mr. Kermit goggles. "A what?"

"A bucket-filler is someone loving and caring, who fills other people's invisible buckets with good wishes and positive reinforcement that make them feel special." She regards Aldo disapprovingly.

"Someone who creates a disturbance and makes it impossible for other children to learn is not a bucket-filler. That's a bucket-*dipper*."

Suddenly, I realize what she's talking about. It's from this picture book that's supposed to teach little kids to be nice to each other. It's really big—in about first grade.

"It's an elementary school thing, Mr. Kermit," Kiana supplies helpfully.

"Just because this is middle school doesn't mean we shouldn't treat one another with *respect*," Miss Fountain says earnestly. "It worked for my kindergarten class last year, and we should have higher expectations for children who are even older. Right, Mr. Kermit?"

I wait for our teacher to give her the brush-off. Good old Ribbit could brush off World War Three. But for some reason, he doesn't. With great effort, he tears his eyes off her and swivels to me. "Were you—*dipping*?"

I stare at my sneakers. "I guess."

Mr. Kermit turns back to Miss Fountain. "You look just like your mother."

She smiles. "I'll take that as a compliment." To me, she says, "You should apologize to your classmates too. You wasted their learning time as well as your own."

"Sorry," I mumble. "You know—about the learning time."

"Relax," Rahim drawls. "Who learns?"

"Thank you, Mr. Kermit," Miss Fountain says uncertainly. "I'll give my mother your regards." She backs out of the room, shutting the door quietly behind her.

"Weird lady," Barnstorm puts in, waving a crutch dismissively. "All that bucket-filler stuff. Like we're six years old."

"Hey!" Mr. Kermit shoots him a sharp glance. "Miss Fountain is not 'weird.' She's a teacher."

"Can't she be both?" Rahim wonders out loud.

Kiana won't let it drop. She's not just bossy; she's nosy too. And the combination makes her like a bloodhound. "What gives, Mr. Kermit? What's the deal with you and Miss Fountain?"

For the first time all year, he actually looks annoyed. "Did I or did I not distribute worksheets?"

A paper airplane does a loop-the-loop in front of him. There's a chorus of *ribbits*, including one from Elaine that sounds like it came from the underworld.

Parker chimes in. "Face it, Mr. K. You've barely looked away from your puzzles since school started. But the minute she shows up, you hit the ceiling."

"She's your kryptonite," Mateo puts in.

Kiana snaps her fingers. "It's her mom, right? You and Miss Fountain's mother used to be a thing."

Mr. Kermit, who couldn't even be riled by a roaring bonfire in his wastebasket, picks up his crossword puzzle, rips it into a million pieces, stomps on them, and stalks out.

Even though I can't stand the guy, at that moment, I actually relate to him a little bit. He may be the worst teacher in the world, but we have something in common.

He has anger management problems too.

# Five

## Mr. Kermit

Emma Fountain! I can scarcely believe it. Of all the classrooms in all the schools, she has to walk into mine!

She's a time machine—that's what she is. The spitting image of her mother. It brings back memories I thought were buried forever.

I can still see the engagement notice in the newspaper—Fiona Bertelsman and Zachary Kermit, the photo of the happy couple cheek to cheek, eyebrows perfectly aligned. Smiling like nothing was ever going to come and rain on our parade. How innocent we were then. How blind. How foolish.

It was all over in a heartbeat. The test. The scandal. The breakup. Since then, I've only seen smiles like that twice: seven months later, when Fiona lined her eyebrows up with Gil Fountain in the engagement notices; and today, when their daughter, Emma, stepped through the doorway of room 117.

Fate has a way of sticking it to you twice, resurfacing like a bad burrito. This morning was my second shot. Every day draws me twenty-four hours closer to early retirement, but the last lap isn't going to be a cakewalk. First Thaddeus and the Unteachables, and now Fiona's clone in the room next door—a living, breathing, bucket-filling reminder of the life I missed out on.

If that poor kid tries to teach middle schoolers the way she ran her kindergarten classes, her students will have her throat open by Columbus Day. I should sit her down and explain a few things, but that would mean I *care*. Caring is where the trouble starts—hard experience taught me that. I didn't make it to the cusp of early retirement by caring. I made it by keeping my head down, regardless of whether they give me honor students or Unteachables or the zombie apocalypse. All I have to do is *endure*.

There are small satisfactions. The hiss of the air-controlled closing of the school entrance behind me as I exit the building. The crunch of my shoes on the bad pavement of the parking lot. The stab of pain in my sore shoulder as I open the ill-fitting door of my 1992 Chrysler Concorde—the one Fiona and I bought to start our new life together. Sky blue, although now it's mostly rust. I don't know why I've kept it so long. For sure it isn't the money. The repair bills alone would have bought me a Lamborghini.

I turn the key in the ignition, and the motor coughs and dies. A few minutes later, the hood is open, and I'm staring in at who knows what. Suddenly, there's a screech of tires and a pickup truck is reversing across the parking lot at top speed, hurtling toward me. My one thought is that, if I'm crushed to death here and now, Dr. Thaddeus and the school district won't ever have to pay for my early retirement.

The pickup roars to a stop with its rear bumper six inches from my legs.

Eyes blazing, I shout, "Are you crazy—?"

The door opens and the driver gets out. I blink. It's one of my *students*! I know the Unteachables are

46

a rough crowd, but I never expected one of them to steal a truck and use it to try to kill me!

"Sorry, the gas pedal sometimes sticks a little." When my shocked expression doesn't fade, the kid adds, "It's me—Parker from class. What can I do to help?"

"To start with," I rasp, "you can stop reversing at ninety miles an hour. Why is a middle schooler driving at all?"

As he launches into a whole story about his grandmother, the family farm, and a provisional license, I conjure up a picture of him in a front-row desk, examining worksheets from point-blank range like he's staring through a jeweler's eyepiece.

"Wow, that's a pretty old car," he tells me. "I mean, *mine's* old, but yours is like—classic." He squints at the name in raised chrome letters. "It's a—Coco Nerd."

"Concorde," I correct impatiently. Didn't anyone ever teach this boy to read? "Never mind that. Any idea how I can get it started up again?"

Give Parker credit—he's better with cars than he is with words. He tinkers around under the hood, and pretty soon the motor is running again, although it's belching gray smoke all over the parking lot.

"Stop it!"

A silver Prius pulls alongside. The window is open,

and through the billowing clouds, we can just make out Miss Emma Fountain.

"Turn it off! Turn it off!"

Parker rushes behind the wheel and kills the engine.

She gets out of the Prius, waving her arms to clear the air. "Do you have any idea how much carbon is in that smoke?"

"Mrs. Vardalos is the chemistry teacher," I reply, deliberately misunderstanding the point she's trying to make. "I'm in charge of—well, you know which class I'm in charge of." I indicate Parker with a slight nod.

"I'm bucket-filling," Parker tells her proudly. "You know, helping Mr. Ribbit—I mean Kermit—"

"Mr. Kermit," she asks, "how *old* is this car?"

"Your mother picked it out," I inform her with an oddly defiant smile.

Her eyes widen. "Oh, wow, that's old. It's just that people didn't understand emissions back then. It was before everyone started putting the environment first—recycling, composting, installing solar panels . . ."

A long speech forms in my mind—about how this is a free country, and it's none of her business what anybody drives, or how old it is, or what it spews into the atmosphere. But for some reason I can't say it. Not to *her*; not to that face that looks so much like Fiona's.

She softens. "Well, maybe you can keep it. But you definitely have to put in a catalytic converter."

"It's on my list," I assure her. "Right after a new floor for the back seat, just in case I ever have passengers."

Parker peers into the back. "Whoa, is that the *ground*?"

"Air-conditioning," I supply, tight-lipped. "Old-school."

Emma regards me with pity.

On the plus side, she and Parker manage to get the motor running again—minus the smoke this time.

"Wow, Miss Fountain," Parker raves. "You're really good with cars."

"I learned from my mom," she explains. "She took a course in auto mechanics because she bought a real lemon once and . . ." Her voice trails off as she frowns at the old Concorde, connecting the dots.

I swallow what's left of my pride. "Thanks for your help." I'm positive that her first act after getting home will be to call her mother and say, *Ma—guess what? He's still got that car. . . .*

The calendar appears in my mind, that magical date in June circled in gold Sharpie.

Only 172 more school days to go.

# Six

## Mateo Hendrickson

**W**hen I get really bored—which is every day—I match people I know with characters from TV and movies. For example, my sister Lauren is like Venom from *Spider-Man* because she's evil and she spits poison. Well, not literally, but since I invented the classification system, I get to choose who's what. Just don't tell my mom, because she's like Professor McGonagall from *Harry Potter*. Smart and usually fair, but she can be nasty when something ticks her off—like me comparing Lauren to a *Spider-Man* villain.

It works for the kids at school too. Parker is like Lightning McQueen because he's the only kid who drives. Barnstorm is the Flash since he was such a great athlete before he wound up on crutches. Rahim is a little tricky, but I think of him as Birdman, because he has really big ears that could easily expand to wings if he gets bitten by a radioactive canary. Crazy, I know, but in comics, that kind of thing happens all the time. Anyway, I can always switch him to Sleeping Beauty. He's not that beautiful, but he is that sleeping.

Elaine is a cross between Chewbacca from *Star Wars* and Lois Lane, who also rhymes with pain. I try not to get too close to her. She once picked a kid up by the belt and used his head to poke at a fluorescent light that was buzzing.

Kiana is Blonde Phantom, since they're both from California, even though Kiana's hair is closer to light brown. And Aldo? That's easy. Dr. Bruce Banner, who turns into the Incredible Hulk when he gets mad.

As for me, I'm part hobbit and part Vulcan—Bilbo and Spock. Big logic in a small package.

That leaves just our teacher, Mr. Kermit. He's tough to characterize. I'm leaning toward Squidward because when he comes to class in the morning, he reminds me of Squidward coming to work at the Krusty Krab—bored and bummed out. And he treats us the way Squidward treats the customers. He doesn't hate us exactly, but he definitely wishes we were someplace else. He's even a little grumpier than Squidward because he doesn't have a hobby like playing the clarinet—unless you count crossword puzzles and consuming mass quantities of coffee.

For someone who's supposed to be a teacher, he sure doesn't do too much teaching. He mostly just hands out worksheets. The only time he talks is when somebody asks a question. That usually ends up being me.

"Mr. Kermit, why do the magnetic poles reverse?"

With effort, the teacher tears his attention away from his puzzle. "Excuse me?"

"Every two hundred and fifty thousand years, Earth's magnetic poles reverse," I explain. "I was just wondering why that happens."

"Yes, but what does it have to do with"—reluctantly, he glances from his *New York Times* to the worksheet on his desk beside it—"using vocabulary words in a sentence?"

"I want to do a sentence on Magneto," I reason. "But since his superpower is magnetism and electric charge, he'd be affected by that."

That's another thing about Mr. Kermit. He isn't very helpful when one of his students is curious about something.

The only other time there are questions is when Parker is trying to figure out what a word is. That turns into kind of a game in SCS-8—figuring out what he means by *tramgulley* when the word is really *metallurgy*. Sometimes the whole class gets in on guessing. It's the only fun we have during school. It can get pretty loud when people start laughing at Parker. Mr. Kermit's usually okay with it, unless Miss Fountain comes over to complain that we're disturbing her class. Then he chews us out. He doesn't get mad at us, but he can't stand it when *she* does.

This one time, Barnstorm makes a big stink, pounding his desk with both crutches, because the football team is holding its first pep rally and he isn't going to be up there with the players. "It's not fair, man!" he roars. "Just because I'm injured doesn't mean I'm not a Golden Eagle!"

Mr. Kermit's curiosity is suddenly piqued. "If you were in the pep rally, you'd have to leave now, right? You'd be somewhere else for the rest of the day?"

Barnstorm nods. "The team gets the whole afternoon

off to prepare for it, and I'm stuck here working."

That might be pushing it a little. I've seldom seen Barnstorm pick up a pencil.

"That sounds reasonable to me," Mr. Kermit agrees. "It isn't your fault you got injured. Why should you have to suffer for it?"

I get the feeling that Mr. Kermit doesn't care that much about justice for Barnstorm. What he really wants is to get this disturber of the peace out of room 117 before he puts one of those crutches through a wall. Miss Fountain would definitely notice that.

So he goes on the intercom and demands to have Barnstorm included in the rally. He argues his way through three secretaries and the assistant principal, and he won't take no for an answer. We're blown away. It's a whole new side to our teacher none of us has seen before. He's actually fighting for one of us, when we would have bet money that he barely even noticed we were here.

"Put me through to Coach Slattery," Mr. Kermit insists.

"He's in class right now" comes the reply from the speaker.

"Well, get him *out* of class," our teacher retorts. "Justice and fairness aren't just part of the social studies curriculum, you know. They're the building blocks of our entire society."

No one is more amazed than Barnstorm himself. "That's what I'm talking about," he approves in a satisfied tone.

By the time Mr. Kermit gets on with the athletic office, he's really worked up. "You ought to be ashamed of yourself!" he accuses Coach Slattery. "You send these kids out there to be tackled and elbowed and hit with hockey sticks. And when they get injured, you abandon them?"

When the coach finally breaks down and says, "Okay, whatever. Send him down," our whole class breaks into applause.

"You were awesome, Mr. Kermit!" Kiana exclaims.

"You should be in the Justice League," I add.

He looks startled, as if he didn't realize anybody was listening. He turns to Barnstorm. "Well, off you go. Enjoy your . . ." His voice trails off.

"Pep rally," I supply helpfully.

Barnstorm is already thump-swinging toward the door. "Thanks, Mr. Kermit."

Throughout the afternoon, our teacher keeps looking at Barnstorm's empty desk and smiling—another first for him. And at the end of the day, when we're called down to the pep rally, he smiles all the way to the auditorium—even though our class is always terrible marching through the hallways. Aldo karate-kicks lockers, and Rahim stakes out a water fountain so he can spray people. This seventh grader gives Elaine a hard time about blocking the stairs but only till he realizes who he's talking to. Better to be blocked on the stairs than to take a one-way trip down them or to have a classroom door slammed on your head or any of the other things Elaine does to people who annoy her. The kid apologizes and gets out of there so fast that he slams into Parker, and they both end up blocking the stairs for real.

Not even that spoils Mr. Kermit's mood. It's a problem. He's much too happy to be Squidward now.

Until we reach the auditorium. We're standing there waiting for our turn to file in when an earsplitting honk goes off right behind us. Mr. Kermit practically hits the ceiling. He wheels around to see this kid with a bright green vuvuzela—one of those noisemakers that look like a long plastic trumpet. They're kind of a tradition for Golden Eagle sports, because one of our school board members is from South Africa, where they were invented.

Without a word, Mr. Kermit snatches the thing out

of the kid's hand, throws it to the floor, and stomps it flat.

The boy looks up at him, lip quivering. "But it's a pep rally."

"Who says pep can't be quiet?" The teacher's furious eyes fix on a girl, who's holding a purple one. "Don't even think about it."

Nervously, she whisks the instrument behind her back.

Mr. Kermit nods. "That's the spirit."

Problem solved; he's Squidward again. When it comes to vuvuzelas, he might even be Lex Luthor.

At the pep rally, they make us sit in the back, just in case we have to be kicked out. Our class always sits in the back, even in the cafeteria. The teachers don't want us anywhere near the soda machine. They think giving us sugar is like sprinkling water on the Gremlins.

I cheer when Barnstorm is introduced. I've never known anybody on a team before. He waves a crutch in our direction, and a few of the other kids clap too.

Then Rahim falls asleep. His head slumps over and conks the girl sitting next to him.

We get kicked out.

# Seven

## Kiana Roubini

'm still in SCS-8.

Well, technically I'm in nothing, since I never officially enrolled in school. Back on the first day, Chauncey turned out to have stomach flu. That's why he barfed—like there needs to be a reason for him to paint the town. So Stepmonster never showed up to register me.

That night, eating takeout pizza for dinner, while feeding Chauncey medicine out of an eyedropper, she asked me, "Kiana, did you get everything straight-ened out with the office?"

"Jeez, Louise!" my father exclaimed. "You were supposed to take care of that."

"Chauncey got sick—" she began defensively.

"It's okay," I interrupted. "It's all taken care of."

I'm still not sure why I said that. Nothing is taken care of. There's no such student as Kiana Roubini at Greenwich Middle School. If I had any teacher besides Mr. Kermit, I would have been busted on day one.

What's more, I'm in the Unteachables. Oh, sure, they call it the Self-Contained Special yada, yada, yada. But that's just code for burnouts, nitwits, rejects, and behavior problems. Plus one displaced Californian.

It goes without saying that I don't belong. I've kind of boxed myself into a corner, though. It wouldn't be hard to switch out, since I was never really switched in. But then I'd need Stepmonster to register me for real. *And* I'd have to explain what I've been doing for the past two weeks.

It's not worth it. I'm a short-timer anyway. I never changed my address from Los Angeles, so no one will ever find out there's a girl living here who isn't enrolled in school. And believe me, Mr. Kermit isn't going to notice he's got an extra kid in his class. Most of the time, he doesn't even notice he's got a class.

I'm not learning anything. But even if I was in genius classes, I don't think there's much this one-horse town can teach me in two months. Could be even less—Mom says her movie is going really well, which means I could be back in California even sooner than expected. Fingers and toes crossed.

In spite of all that, I have to admit I'm fascinated by SCS-8. It's not a good class—not even close. It's kind of an interesting one, though. I always assumed that kids who end up in programs like that are just plain dumb. Not this bunch. They have quirks, sure. But unteachable? I don't see what's so terrible about them that they can't be with everybody else. Well, maybe Aldo. Anybody who can get that mad at a locker, and all that. Still, when I look into Aldo's eyes—which are green, by the way—I see a person who doesn't want to be so angry.

Anyway, if the kids are a little strange, they're not half as strange as their teacher. I use the word *teacher* very loosely. That's another problem I have about calling them the Unteachables. How can the school know they're unteachable if nobody ever tries to teach them?

It's been two weeks and Mr. Kermit hasn't taught anything yet. He barely even speaks. He doesn't like kids, and he doesn't seem too fond of other adults either. Yet there's something cool about him too. Nothing throws him, except maybe vuvuzelas. Anybody who could put out a trash can bonfire with a cup of coffee and never mention it must have ice water in his veins—even by LA standards.

And just when you think you've got him figured out, something new about him comes out. Like his secret past with Miss Fountain's mother. Or when he fought like a tiger to get Barnstorm included in the pep rally. Now Barnstorm is fully reinstated to the Golden Eagles. He even stands on the sidelines at football games, leaning on his crutches and dispensing advice to the players. He has Mr. Kermit to thank for that.

One day, Barnstorm is off at a team meeting when Miss Fountain pokes her head into the room.

"Mr. Kermit," she calls, "my group is about to have Circle Time, and we were wondering if you and your students might like to join us."

"Circle Time?" he repeats, mystified.

I stare at our teacher. How could anybody in the school business never have heard about Circle Time? "You know," I explain, "like the little kids do."

"It's not just for little kids," Miss Fountain corrects.

"It's for everybody. Positive reinforcement is something you never outgrow. Think of how much better our world would be if national leaders would only sit in a circle and be kind and civil to one another."

So we all troop over to room 115, and let me tell you, that class doesn't look too thrilled to see us coming in the door. They're seventh graders—only a year younger than us—but it's a major year for growth spurts, so they seem a lot punier. Plus, we have a reputation—that was obvious from the VIP seats they gave us at the pep rally, and how quickly we got thrown out at the first sign of trouble.

Miss Fountain's students are intimidated by all of us, so you can imagine how they feel about Elaine, the subject of school legends about force-feeding people pages of their own textbooks and pounding them with uprooted ficus trees. Plus, she covers literally thirty degrees of the whole circle. There really is a circle, marked off with yellow tape on the floor. In the middle is a smiley face, also in yellow tape. If my friends in LA could see me now. On second thought, God forbid. Kid drivers, Unteachables, and now this. Greenwich sure is some town.

Mr. Kermit doesn't want to sit on the floor with the kids, but Miss Fountain does it, so he has to do it too.

There's a lot of groaning as he lowers himself down, and a crack that might be from a hip joint. He balances the bucket of coffee precariously on his lap.

The room is like an overgrown kindergarten class. Bright colors blaze from every wall. There are class lists with multicolored stars awarded. Every single piece of information comes in a voice bubble emerging from the mouth of a happy cartoon animal—Suzy the Science Snake and Harvey the Hall Pass Hippo. I'd probably like it—if I was about Chauncey's age. Mateo *does* like it. He lives his life through fictional characters anyway. He lingers in front of the big posters, drinking in the details of the vibrant caricatures. Mr. Kermit has to order him to take a seat on the circle.

Miss Fountain even has a *real* animal. In a glass terrarium in the corner of the room, under a sign proclaiming him to be VLADIMIR, is some kind of lizard about eight inches long.

"A miniature Gorn!" Mateo blurts.

"He's a gecko," a seventh grader corrects.

Parker snaps his fingers. "Like that lizard from the TV commercials."

"He's a gold dust day gecko," Miss Fountain explains. "You can tell by the flecks of yellow in his scales."

"Gorns are from *Star Trek*," Mateo supplies, although nobody asked for an explanation. "They're a reptilian race from Tau Lacertae 9, advanced enough to have mastered space travel."

A loud snicker comes from one of the seventh graders.

"Class, let's welcome our new friends to the circle," Miss Fountain announces. "Who has a compliment to offer?"

"Somebody's feet stink," Aldo complains.

Mr. Kermit glares at him. "That's not a compliment!"

"Yeah, I know," Aldo concedes, "but something smells pretty ripe around here."

"Maybe it's the Gorn cage," Mateo puts in.

"A compliment," Miss Fountain goes on as if no one else has spoken, "is a positive comment, a 'well done!' to make people feel good about themselves. Try again, Aldo."

Aldo is thinking so hard that his face screws up, like Chauncey's when he's going to the bathroom in his diaper. He looks all around the circle and comes up empty.

I know I'm just a short-timer and it's pointless to care about people I'll never have to see again once

Mom finishes shooting her movie. But my heart goes out to Aldo, who has this red, red hair that just won't stay combed. How must it feel inside when the closest you can get to saying something nice involves foot odor?

From the opposite side of the room, a low voice announces, "That's a nice color."

We all crane our necks to see who's speaking. To my amazement, it's *Elaine*!

"I beg your pardon," says the young teacher, distracted.

"Your shirt," Elaine tells Miss Fountain. "It's a nice look for you."

"What a lovely thing to say! Thank you—" Miss Fountain frowns at Elaine. "I don't think I know your name."

"I don't think so either," Elaine rumbles back.

Miss Fountain turns questioningly to Mr. Kermit, who gives her a blank shrug.

"That's Elaine!" I exclaim. We've been in class with him for two weeks. Doesn't he know any of us?

A few whispered murmurs of "rhymes with pain" come from our class and the seventh graders.

A voice sounds in the hall. "Where'd everybody go?" A moment later, Barnstorm swings into the doorway on his crutches, fresh from his meeting with the football team. "I was wondering where you guys—hey, check it out! Circle Time!"

"Join our circle," Miss Fountain invites. "Why don't you share how you hurt your leg? I'm guessing it was a football injury."

"No way," Barnstorm scoffs. "The tackler isn't born who can catch me. I was changing a lightbulb in the bathroom and I slipped off the toilet seat."

I can see it coming, but I'm powerless to stop it. As Barnstorm plops himself down on the floor next to Aldo, one of his crutches whacks the red-haired boy in the side of the head.

"Ow!" Enraged, Aldo sweeps the offending crutch aside, knocking it into the corner. The rubber tip clips the cover on the lizard terrarium, sending it skittering across the floor.

"The Gorn!" Mateo exclaims.

"Vladimir!" cry several of the seventh graders.

The gecko is out of his home like a shot. He does a quick loop of the room and finds the door, posthaste.

Mateo frowns. "Gorns are slow and plodding in *Star Trek*."

"I guess *Star Trek* isn't that much like real life," Parker observes.

You can say that again. There's nothing slow or lazy about Vladimir. By the time the first seventh graders reach the hall, their class pet is long gone.

I'm kind of impressed by how calm Miss Fountain stays. She's all business on the intercom with the office describing the escaped lizard.

"Thank you for a very enjoyable—uh, Circle Time," Mr. Kermit says formally. "We should probably say our goodbyes, though."

I doubt she even hears him.

Back in room 117, I'm thinking now we're really going to get it. But our teacher silently returns to his crossword puzzle, leaving us to the worksheets on our desks.

# Eight
## Mr. Kermit

**W**hen breakfast is mustard on toast, that's a sure sign that it's time to go back to the grocery store. It means I've run out of butter and cream cheese and jam, and I'm digging into the condiment packs left over from my last McDonald's run. Come to think of it, this is my last slice of bread too, and stale doesn't begin to describe it.

The apartment is a dump—clean enough, but definitely from a bygone era. I can afford much better, but I'm too disinterested to redecorate and too lazy to move. It's the perfect place for a meal of mustard on toast—the breakfast of the disinterested and lazy. Not for the first time, I picture Fiona's house, with its picket fence and oh-so-green lawn. It's more vivid now, since I can imagine Emma growing up there, playing on the swings, riding her tricycle on the driveway, and playing with her first lizard. I don't want to think about her *last* lizard, thanks to the Unteachables. God only knows what happened to Vladimir. He's probably trapped in the walls of the school somewhere, starving to death. If he made it out of the building, he's roadkill for sure.

Eventually, I go down to the Coco Nerd and start it up in a cloud of burnt oil. I'm actually calling it that, thanks to Parker. For some reason, I can't get it out of my head. Something else to lay at the feet of the Unteachables.

June has never looked farther away.

I'm not even a third of the way to school when the billboard looms up:

COME SEE THE LARGEST INVENTORY OF
NEW AND USED
VEHICLES IN THE TRI-COUNTY AREA

And there's his face, grinning out through a flaming hoop like he's some kind of circus performer and not the sleazy used-car dealer he was always meant to be. Jumping Jake Terranova, who will jump through hoops to get you a great deal on the perfect new or used car.

Even though I pass this billboard every day, it's always somehow a blow to see him up there. He doesn't look much different than he did as a seventh grader. Always grinning, like he's got it all figured out. And he's still selling—cars and SUVs now, instead of stolen copies of the National Aptitude Test. He's good at it too. Terranova Motors is the third-largest auto dealership in the state. That's quite an accomplishment. Jumping Jake has come a long way since seventh grade, when his biggest accomplishment was ruining his teacher's life.

No, I remind myself, Dr. Thaddeus did that. Sure, the cheating thing was an ugly scandal, but it's not as if I was in on the scam. All I was guilty of was trusting my students—and believing that their best-in-the-nation test score was an honest achievement.

My *real* crime—the one I'll never be forgiven for—was making Thaddeus *look bad*. The principal-turned-superintendent has been taking his revenge ever since. Jake Terranova was just the first tile that started the dominoes tumbling.

The giant dealership looms up on the left. I can't help it—I count how long it takes to pass the vast lots and showrooms. Fourteen full seconds at the speed of traffic. It isn't enough that the Terranova kid got away with his seventh-grade shenanigans; obviously, they gave him the formula for getting rich. He's rolling in money while the teacher he took down is living on bread and mustard and driving a Coco Nerd— although the main reason I haven't replaced the car is that I blame all auto dealerships for Jake Terranova.

I turn into the school lot where Parker's pickup truck is sprawled across the last two open spaces. Sure, give a middle school kid a driver's license. What could go wrong? Annoyed, I block the pickup in, making a mental note to keep the kid after school just long enough to beat him out here.

I didn't pack a lunch, but I remember buying a falafel a couple of days ago that I never got around to eating. It isn't on the passenger seat, so I try the glove compartment. No luck. It must have fallen on the floor and rolled under the seat when the car went over a bump. The Coco Nerd doesn't have much in the way of suspension.

Bending over double, I reach around and pat the floor on the passenger side. Sure enough, I find the paper sack. But when I pull it out, there's a hole in the bag, and the falafel is half-eaten and torn to shreds.

I get on all fours and peer under the seat. It looks like somebody lost a leather wallet down there. Then it shifts, and two beady eyes peer out at me.

I recoil in shock, slamming the back of my head against the dashboard. With a squeak of fear, the creature begins to scramble away, but I jam my hand in and grab it before it can escape through the hole in the floor.

Breathing hard, I draw the little guy out and hold him against my chest. "Vladimir, I presume."

In answer, the gecko poops on my shirt. I sigh, unable to muster up any anger or even surprise. Vladimir is merely continuing a pattern of treatment that's been going on for twenty-seven years. I brush the tiny pellets away.

So the fugitive lizard *did* make it out of the building. Not only that, but he managed to find the one car in the parking lot with a hole in the floor and a falafel just waiting to be feasted on. And he's been here for the past eighteen hours, safe and sound while the custodians scoured the school, listening to every wall with stethoscopes.

Still toting the little beast, I get out of the car. I hold on pretty tight at first, but relax when I realize Vladimir isn't going anywhere. Why should he? He's eating the rest of my lunch as we enter the school.

I'm actually looking forward to restoring Vladimir to his rightful owner. True, that's dangerously close to caring. But Emma is almost like my daughter from an alternate universe, her being Fiona's kid. The young teacher already thinks my class is a horde of barbarians—mostly because they are. This might get her to consider the possibility that I'm not to blame for it.

As I approach room 115, her voice stops me in my tracks.

"I know teachers get burned-out, Mom, but this is different. He's barely even alive! I teach right next door to him. He doesn't open his mouth all day! Those poor kids are going to learn nothing because nobody's there to teach them! It's such a shame . . ."

I back up a step. She's stalking around the room, updating her bulletin boards with gold stars, holding her phone to her ear with one hunched shoulder. What she's saying hurts all the more because of who she's saying it to.

A surge of resentment. What does Emma Fountain

know about being burned-out? She's barely older than the students. She thinks giving middle schoolers gold stars and class pets and lecturing them about being bucket-fillers is education. How long has she been teaching—ten minutes? The first time she tried to take on the Unteachables, they laid waste to her circle and released her lizard to the four winds.

But Fiona's never going to hear *that* side of the story.

Emma adjusts a drooping nostril on Harvey the Hall Pass Hippo. "Okay, fine, he used to be a great teacher once. It's *now* that counts! Honestly, I can't believe you were actually *engaged* to that—"

I tense up, giving the gecko a squeeze. A short, sharp squeak is torn from his little mouth.

She wheels, and the phone drops from her ear.

*"Vladimir!"* She grabs the lost pet from my arms and rains kisses down on his scaly head. "Where did you find him?"

"Around," I reply stiffly. I'm not in the mood for a conversation about the hole in the back of my car.

She's red in the face now. "How long have you been standing there, Mr. Kermit?"

I'm tempted to say, "Long enough," or something else to make her feel bad, because she of all people

should know that wasn't a very bucket-filling conversation. But I hold my tongue.

This used to be my favorite part of the day—when
the students haven't come yet to ruin it. It's usually
downhill from there.

My dramatic exit is spoiled by a small mustard burp
as breakfast climbs a little higher up the back of my
throat.

I need coffee. I cheer myself by picturing the Toilet
Bowl on the shelf in the faculty lounge, dwarfing all
the lesser mugs.

# Nine

## Parker Elias

**B**ack when Grandpa was alive, he and Grams ran the lunch counter at the bus station. I can still picture the LUNCHEONETTE sign, which always looked like ELECT THE NOUN to me. I don't remember much about Grandpa except that he used to tell me it was a "ten-dollar word" and I'd be able to read it just fine when I got older. (We know how that worked out.)

Grams would stand me up in front of the candy

counter, which seemed like it was a mile high—although that was just because I was small. She'd say, "What'll it be, kiddo?" and I could pick out whatever I wanted.

In those days, I didn't mind being "kiddo," because she definitely knew my real name. "This handsome fellow is my grandson, Parker!" she'd announce whenever the regulars came by. You could just tell by the way she boomed it out that she was totally thrilled by the idea.

I wonder if she knows that the guy who drives her every morning is the same little kid she used to brag about to her customers. It's not her fault—when Grandpa died, she started forgetting a lot of stuff. But you'd think a grandson could be an exception to that—especially a grandson who's supposed to be her favorite person in the whole world.

Grams insists that the reason she can't get her act together is she isn't a morning person. This from a lady who gets up at four a.m. So we'll be halfway to the senior center before I look down and notice that her shoes don't match, or that instead of her purse, she brought a half loaf of Wonder bread. There are those red, yellow, and blue polka dots smiling up at me, along with the name, which looks like DOWNER.

Today Mom's driving because Grams has her

semiannual conference with the social worker at the senior center. Mom calls it Meet the Teacher, since I guess it's a lot like a parent conference at school.

"Speaking of which," she says to me, "how's eighth grade going? I understand you're in a different kind of program this year."

I almost reply, "Yeah, the Unteachables." But that wouldn't be a good idea. The minute she got through with *Grams's* Meet the Teacher, she'd be stalking the middle school looking to meet *my* teacher. I picture my folks trying to hold a conversation with Ribbit, who never glances up from his crossword puzzle. Dad, especially, would have no patience for that. Fall is our busiest season on the farm, with so much harvesting still to do.

So I tell her, "It's going fine, like always."

She casts me a doubtful look. *Like always* might not have been the best choice of words. Mom signs my report cards. She knows better than anyone what *like always* probably means.

I add, "Our teacher has a lot of experience." He started out teaching stegosauruses and pterodactyls before moving on to Unteachables. Dinosaurs had no problem being in class with a guy who did crossword puzzles all day.

Mom looks like she has more questions, but luckily, Grams is waiting outside her building—no mismatched clothes or missing socks, no rubber gasket from the coffeemaker on her wrist instead of her medical-alert bracelet. She's thrown a little to see me in the passenger seat instead of behind the wheel, so it takes some coaxing to get her into the truck. She has to sit on the hump between Mom and me, since the pickup has no back seat.

"Of all the cars, you picked this one?" she asks Mom. "You're crazy."

"It's just for a couple of minutes," my mother promises. "Once we drop Parker at school, you'll have plenty of room."

"*I'm* Parker," I put in quickly, since Grams is looking around the car in confusion.

She beams at me. "Hiya, kiddo! Want breakfast?"

"No time. We're coming up on my stop."

Mom pulls up in front of the school and I get out. She waves. "Have fun."

Yeah, right. *Fun*—that's the last word that comes to mind when I think of SCS-8. On the other hand, a sit-down with Grams and a social worker won't be a party either. I'm probably getting the better deal.

As the pickup roars off, I hear a crunching sound.

79

A crushed vuvuzela lies on the pavement, the plastic busted by the weight of the truck. It seems like there are more of them around every day as we get closer to Spirit Week. And these are just leftovers from last year. The word is that Principal Vargas just placed this giant order of new ones for 2019. They're going to be bright yellow—our school color—and say *Go, Go, Golden Eagles* on the side. It doesn't make much sense to me that you can get a detention for chewing gum, but blasting away on a horn as loud as an air raid siren is considered school spirit.

Instead of being late like most other mornings, I've got the opposite problem. I'm early. The buses haven't started arriving yet. I wander down to room 117, but nobody's there. The kids of SCS-8 dribble in ten seconds before the late bell, and at that, we're usually ahead of Mr. Kermit. The only signs of life are coming from the room next door: 115.

Miss Fountain is in her classroom, rearranging the Velcro smiley faces on her job boards. There's already a Hershey's Kiss sitting in the middle of each desk. You know what Mr. Kermit gives us every morning? Nothing—if you don't count the dirty looks.

She spots me standing there in the doorway. "Good

morning, Parker. You're early today. Come have a kiss."

I stare at her for a long time before I realize she's talking about the candy. "Uh—thanks." The chocolate is sweet in my mouth. When you spend all your time in SCS-8, you almost forget there's another way to live.

My eyes find the lizard terrarium. "Hey," I say suddenly. "Vladimir's back!"

She beams. "Mr. Kermit found him for me."

"Really?" That doesn't sound like the Ribbit I know—the one who wouldn't give anybody the skin off a grape.

Suddenly, I experience an almost irresistible desire to drop to the floor and sit cross-legged on the taped circle. I know Miss Fountain's teaching style is too babyish for our age, but Circle Time that day might have been the most comfortable I've ever felt in middle school. When you're in that circle, nobody's going to ask you to read something that's written in Unbreakable Code. Maybe Aldo can't come up with any nice things to say, but I'm willing to go with it. If it means no reading, I'll even say nice things about Elaine.

A couple of the seventh graders show up, and there's an emotional reunion with Vladimir. I join in for a while, but eventually one of them notices I'm there.

"*You're* not in this class," he comments meaningfully.

That's right, I reflect with a sigh. I'm not. I shoulder my backpack and head next door, even though it's still early.

Kiana crouches in the hall outside SCS-8, a look of intense concentration on her face.

"What's going on?" I ask.

"Shhh!" She presses a finger to her lips and points inside the classroom.

Mr. Kermit is talking, and at first I think he's chewing someone out. His voice is a lot sharper than his usual half-sleepy drone. Then I hear the reply—tinny and very close. It's coming from the intercom, right on the other side of the door. Principal Vargas.

"I'd think you'd be happy about this, Zachary," the principal is saying. "It's no secret that the sound of those vuvuzelas drives you over the edge."

Zachary. Mr. Kermit's name is Zachary.

"That's not the point," our teacher replies. "You've already separated my class from everybody else in the building. Maybe you have your reasons for that. But you can't exclude them from the activities for Spirit Week. That's punishing them for something they haven't done yet."

"You loathe Spirit Week," Mrs. Vargas accuses.

"We're not talking about me. We're talking about my students. As happy as I'd be to ignore the whole thing, I'm their only teacher. Who's going to stick up for them if I don't?"

Beside me, Kiana pumps a fist and whispers, "Go, Ribbit!"

"Think of who we're talking about here," the principal insists. "Think of the disruption they're capable of. Now picture them with vuvuzelas in their hands."

"Let that be my problem," Mr. Kermit says stubbornly.

"It's not going to be anybody's problem," Mrs. Vargas insists. "It's a done deal, Zachary. Your kids are out."

We hear a click as the office breaks the connection. On the other side of the door, Mr. Kermit mutters something I can't make out.

"Did you hear that?" Kiana breathes. "Mr. Kermit cares about us!"

"I didn't hear anything about caring," I retort.

"That was all about vuvuzelas—which we're not getting anyway."

"Weren't you paying attention? He *fought* for us!"

"I can't figure him out," I complain. "He hates vuvuzelas. Why would he want us to have them? So he can kill whoever blows one?"

She throws up her hands in exasperation. "Don't you see? It's not about the noisemakers. It's about *fairness*!"

That doesn't make much sense to me. If life was fair, there would be no such thing as the Unteachables in the first place.

# Ten

## Kiana Roubini

**B**ad news from Utah—the equipment trailer got struck by lightning, so production on my mom's movie has to be shut down for a couple of weeks.

"Can't I come back home while you guys are waiting to start up again?" I ask Mom over Skype.

"That wouldn't work," she tells me. "What about school? How can we pull you out of Greenwich when you just got started? And then re-enroll you once shooting resumes here? That would be too disruptive."

I have to hold myself back from screaming: *There's nothing to disrupt! I don't really go here! Jeez-Louise never registered me! I'm not even in a real class!*

Forget it. Mom would be on the phone to Dad in seconds flat—never a pleasant convo. I'd be back in that office fast enough to make my head spin, registering for eight classes instead of just one. Eight new teachers to get used to—who give real assignments and real homework.

No. My life here isn't perfect, but it's designed for maximum bearableness. Why get complicated? I'm a short-timer—just not quite as short as I thought.

Two extra weeks in Greenwich. Of Dad and Step-monster. Of Chauncey's sniffles and fevers and rashes and barfs.

Two more weeks in the Parmesan House. Two more weeks of the Unteachables.

Fine. I can handle it. I can do two more weeks standing on my head.

"Speaking of school," Mom goes on, "how are you fitting in? I went there, you know—back when it was the old Greenwich High."

"Great," I tell her. "I've already gotten picked for this special program."

Mom beams. "Special?" I knew she wouldn't be

able to resist the idea of me being exceptional.

I plow forward. "It's called SCS-8. Really hard to get into." I should know. I'm not even really in it. "The teacher is fantastic. He's super hands-off because he wants us to learn to work independently. Mr. Kermit believes—"

"Kermit?" she interrupts. "You mean from the cheating scandal?"

"Cheating scandal?"

Mom's brow furrows. "It was an awfully long time ago—the early nineties. I remember I was away at college when it happened. But it must be the same person. Kermit isn't a very common name."

I'm intrigued. "What did Mr. Kermit do?"

"I don't remember the details. But the whole town was up in arms about it. I'm surprised he's still teaching. It was a horrible black mark against him."

Wow—Mr. Kermit has a *past*. The plot thickens.

Mom adds, "Do you want me to call the school and get to the bottom of it?"

"No!" I blurt. "I mean, Mr. Kermit's an awesome teacher *now*, and that's the main thing, right? Who cares what happened in the nineties?"

"But, Kiana—it was a *cheating* scandal! I don't want you mixed up in something like that."

"Relax, Mom," I assure her. "I guarantee that there isn't any cheating going on in SCS-8." I can say that with total confidence because there isn't anything going on, period. Why would we bother to cheat when Mr. Kermit never even looks at the few papers he gets?

Eventually, she agrees to let the subject drop. I end the Skype call, my mind racing. Suddenly, I've cracked a mystery that's been nagging at me from the very first moment I followed Parker's schedule into room 117: Why would Mr. Kermit want to teach a class like the Unteachables?

Answer: he doesn't. He gets a bad class every year because of what happened way back in the nineties. Seems a little crazy that he's still paying for a mistake from so long ago. But if Mom remembers, other people do too.

Turns out SCS-8 isn't just a dumping ground for the rejects of the school. The reject teachers wind up there too.

So Mr. Kermit is famous. If Mom still remembers what he did way back when, that counts as fame. Okay, it was a bad thing, but so what? On reality TV shows, the biggest stars are always the jerks.

Besides, cheating scandal or not, I can't forget how he spoke up for our class to Mrs. Vargas. And how he fought for Barnstorm's right to stay with the football team. He may not be much of a teacher, but I'm more convinced than ever that he's one of the good guys.

I'm almost anxious to get to school the next day, and it isn't just because Chauncey is barking the house down with whooping cough. When I get to room 117, though, Mr. Kermit is absent. We have a substitute, Mrs. Landsman.

Mr. Kermit's not exactly a young guy, but Mrs. Landsman is really old. Rahim does a quick sketch of her, rising from the grave as part of a zombie apocalypse—the kid is really talented. The picture makes the rounds of the class by paper airplane.

"Dawn of the Dead!" hisses Mateo when the portrait lands on his desk.

"No talking!" Mrs. Landsman orders.

Too late. A nickname is born. She's Dawn of the Dead—Dawn for short.

She's grouchy, but we should be used to that by now, our regular teacher being a gold medalist at the Grouch Olympics. It feels different, though. Dawn crabs *at* us, while Mr. Kermit just crabs because crabbing is his natural state. So when some of it lands on us, we don't take it personally. We just happen to be in the same room.

Dawn is yammering on about the Battle of Gettysburg when I hear a power hum, low but growing in volume. At first, I'm afraid the school is about to blow up. Then I realize the sound is coming from the desk next to me—Aldo. His face is almost as red as his hair as he devotes all his breath to maintaining the sound.

Now the hum is coming from behind me, at a slightly different pitch. I risk a glance over my shoulder. Barnstorm's doing it too, a look of unholy glee on his face. Next, the noise drops at least an octave—Elaine, buzzing like a bassoon.

Well, we Californians know how to prank a sub as well as anybody. So I jump right in. Pretty soon, SCS-8 is vibrating.

Alarmed, Dawn of the Dead puts in a call to the custodian. As soon as Mr. Carstairs comes in, we stop humming.

"It was happening just a second ago," the substitute teacher insists. "It sounded like a problem with the wiring."

The custodian rakes us with a rueful look. "It's the kids, ma'am. They're messing with you. They do it to all the subs."

Dawn doesn't like that. For a minute there, I'm afraid we're going to have a real zombie apocalypse on our hands. But in the end, what can she do besides yell? She does a whole lot of that. It's pretty jarring when you're used to Mr. Kermit, who barely speaks at all.

We fight back. We do the old drop-a-textbook trick at least twenty times. Barnstorm drums with his crutches on the floor. Elaine pretends to be asleep, which is odd because Rahim stays awake and alert. Mateo speaks to the substitute in Dothraki and does all his written work in Elven Runes.

That's right, I said work. Dawn of the Dead is trying to run this like an actual *class*. Who does she think she is?

"Take out your math books," she announces.

"What math books?" Barnstorm returns.

"Surely, there are math books." Her frustration is growing. "How do you study math?"

"We do worksheets," Mateo supplies.

"*What* worksheets? I don't see any worksheets! There should be lesson plans—"

Of course there should—*if* we had a normal teacher. But Dawn of the Dead doesn't know Mr. Kermit. Maybe she thinks we ransacked the classroom before she arrived and threw out all the notes on how she was supposed to run the day. Whatever the reason, she's getting madder and madder.

With no lesson plans to go by, Dawn finds a language arts paragraph in some random book. But then she chooses Parker to read it aloud. So obviously, he takes forever to sound out the first word. And because we've been giving her a hard time all day, she picks now to decide that somebody's yanking her chain—when Parker's the only one who isn't. So she sends him to the principal's office. Sixty seconds later, we hear a pickup truck with a broken muffler start up and peel out of the parking lot.

"You know, he didn't do that on purpose," I tell Dawn. "He has a reading problem and he's sensitive about it."

Miss Fountain comes over and tries to calm everybody down by inviting us for another Circle Time.

"Circle Time?" Dawn is outraged. "These students are too old for Circle Time—and so are yours."

Miss Fountain seems to be about to launch into her speech on how no one is too old for positive reinforcement. But then she takes a good look at Dawn of the Dead, who actually might be. She beats a hasty retreat to her own class.

When the bell finally rings at three-thirty, Dawn

of the Dead tells us we're the most disrespectful class she's ever met in her long teaching career, and we should all be ashamed of ourselves. "My son went to this school. He's a successful journalist today, and he'd be appalled to see what's become of the place that gave him his education. You students are a new low. I don't think you'd ever behave for Mr. Kermit the way you behaved today."

As we listen to her sensible heels clicking down the hall, a strange quiet descends in room 117.

"Yeah, well, maybe Mr. Kermit isn't a cranky old bag, like you," Aldo tosses after her when she's too far away to hear it.

"The thing is, she's right," Rahim muses, brow furrowed. "We *wouldn't* behave that way for Ribbit. I wonder why."

I could have answered that. Because even though Mr. Kermit kind of ignores us, he knows we're his class and he sticks up for us when we need it. He *likes* us—in his way. And I'd never be able to explain it to the others, but I think—in our way—we might be starting to like him too.

When Mr. Kermit enters room 117 the next morning, he's greeted by a sight he's never seen before—the seven of us, quiet and attentive, seated at our desks, hands folded, eyes front. Let's face it, there's no way Dawn of the Dead said anything good about us yesterday. This, then, is Payback Time, and none of us are looking forward to it. You can feel the tension in the air as we wait for our teacher to let us have it.

Mr. Kermit sets his newspaper and his coffee down on his desk and looks from face to face. "What?"

Nobody answers, so he starts handing out the first worksheet of the day. The instant the papers hit our desks, there's a pen in every hand and all heads are down.

Out of the corner of my eye, I see the teacher pull up short, frowning. This is another first—the entire class hard at work, no airplanes circling overhead, no talking. He shrugs and returns to his desk, peering down at the crossword puzzle.

I turn my attention to the assignment, which is about current events, and I think hard about what I've seen lately in the news, on the Internet, and in social media.

The intercom buzzes to life. "Mr. Kermit," comes the voice of the secretary, "Principal Vargas is available this morning if you'd like to discuss Mrs. Landsman's report on your students from yesterday."

You can almost hear the jarring sound of a needle scratching across a vinyl record. We all freeze, staring up at our teacher. If Dawn of the Dead filed a report, you can bet she gave us a Z-minus-minus.

"No," Mr. Kermit replies. "Thanks anyway."

That gets our attention. Is Mr. Kermit so detached from reality that he doesn't think anything that happened yesterday was bad? Or is it that he never read Dawn's report, just like he never reads any of our work? The mood in room 117 lightens a little. Whatever the reason, it looks as if we might be off the hook.

It occurs to me that maybe Mr. Kermit never reads our stuff because none of the Unteachables ever hand in anything worth reading. That's an easy fix. There's an essay question on the back of today's worksheet, and I make up my mind to knock it out of the park. The prompt is about mass transit—subways, buses, and light-rail trains. I believe in that kind of thing anyway—I'm from LA, where our transit systems are a joke, and what do we get for it? Traffic jams and pollution. Pretty soon the entire page is full, and I'm only getting started.

I approach Mr. Kermit's desk. Ribbit has pushed his puzzle aside. He's examining a memo from the office. I catch the heading—REPORT OF SUBSTITUTE

TEACHER—across the top. He notices me and I search his eyes for any reaction to what has to be a horrible rundown of her day with a class of unteachable barbarians.

"Are you really mad at us?" I ask in a small voice.

He looks like the question never occurred to him. "There are two sides to every story," he says finally. He reaches down and slides the report into the trash can.

"Is there something I can do for you?" he adds, obviously wishing I would go away.

"Can I have more paper?"

His brow furrows. "For what?"

"My essay. I ran out of space."

That causes kind of a stir in our class. In SCS-8, kids do too little work, never too much.

Mr. Kermit's back into his puzzle now. It's almost as if he's hoping I'll forget what I asked for and leave him alone.

"So can I have it?" I persist.

He looks blank.

"The paper."

"Yes—fine."

"Well, where is it?"

He gets up from his desk and surveys the room, and

it's like he's suddenly found himself in some strange and exotic location—a place he's never seen before. He leads me to a storage closet and opens the door. Empty, except for the cobwebs.

He turns to me, completely helpless.

"Maybe Miss Fountain has extra paper," I suggest.

"I'm on it!" Parker bolts for the door so suddenly that he knocks over his desk and goes flying. He face-plants on the floor, springs right back up, and disappears into the hall.

The next thing we hear is Miss Fountain's voice from the next room: "Parker—you're bleeding!"

"He has a *driver's* license?" Barnstorm sneers. "The kid can barely *walk*."

Parker's back a few minutes later, holding a wad of pink-stained paper towels to his bloody nose. He hands me a sheaf of lined paper, also pink-stained.

I fill four full pages before I'm done with my essay, and I'm pretty satisfied with it. I know I'm just a short-timer, but I can't let my work habits go totally down the drain while I'm here. I'm going to have to be ready to hit the ground running when I get back to my real school in California.

I march up to the front to hand my paper in to Mr. Kermit. He looks at me like I've just presented him with a plate of baby scorpions.

"It's my essay," I reply to the question he probably won't ask. "I can't wait to hear what you think."

He accepts the papers, places them on the corner of the desk, and goes back to his crossword.

"Aren't you going to read it?" I press.

"Of course," he assures me without looking up.

Three days later, the pages still sit on the corner of the desk, untouched.

Parker's blood spots are turning brown.

# Eleven

## Barnstorm Anderson

Thanks to Ribbit, I'm still on the Golden Eagles. It's the nicest thing any teacher ever did for me. Not that I love teachers so much. It's their fault I'm in SCS-8.

I'm not unteachable and I'm definitely not stupid. I'm like any other kid—I can learn, but if you give me the choice not to, I'll pick that. They were totally cool with letting me slide so long as the trophies kept coming. But now that I can't play anymore, all of a sudden my grades aren't up to scratch. Funny how that wasn't a problem last year, when I beasted in three sports.

I load up my tray in the food line and hobble out to the cafeteria—it's not easy to balance a big lunch when you're on crutches. As I scan the tables, this seventh-grade girl I don't know—real cute—smiles and waves at me. This happens to athletes a lot. We're kind of celebrities around school.

I'm trying to figure out how to wave back without dropping either my tray or a crutch, when her gaze veers off to my left. She's not looking at me at all! She's waving to *Karnosky*, one of my teammates on the Golden Eagles, who's coming up beside me!

It's like a gut punch. Karnosky the scrub, who never even got off the bench before I landed on the injured list! Now he's somebody and I'm somebody you look right through.

"'Sup, Anderson," he mumbles, stepping in front of me. He and the girl connect and take the last two spots at the front table—the best location. Last year, half a dozen people would have scrambled to make room for Barnstorm Anderson. Not anymore.

I can take a hint. I'm a Golden Eagle, but not really. What have I done for them lately? If I can't put points on the board today, I'm dead to them.

Not even Ribbit can change *that*.

I keep on hobbling, head held high. I'll die before I let them see I care. It stinks that just moving across the cafeteria has to be a major operation. The way I could *move* used to be what made me who I am. I guess that means I'm nobody—at least till next year.

Another problem: I've hung out with jocks for so long, I've got nowhere else to go. I set my lunch down next to Aldo and Rahim. As I lean my crutches against the side of the table, one of them tips over and whacks Aldo in the shoulder.

"Hey!" he barks angrily.

"Chill out! It was an accident."

It wasn't an accident.

In my athlete days, my mind was always on the field or on the court, juking and cutting, faking imaginary defenders out of their jockstraps. Now that I'm off sports, I don't do that anymore, and my poor mind has nothing to focus on. So I spend my time thinking of ways to get a rise out of Aldo. It's almost too easy.

Aldo is halfheartedly eating a bowl of split pea soup while gazing over at Kiana, who's a few tables away, sitting with Mateo and Parker. That's the rest of SCS-8 except for Elaine, who eats alone, surrounded by a buffer zone of empty tables. People have been keeping their distance from her ever since she chucked this kid into the salad bar. Even in the lunchroom, Elaine rhymes with pain.

While Aldo's staring at Kiana, I reach over and dump half a shaker of black pepper into his soup. I can't help it. It's almost not my fault.

Rahim snickers and doodles a napkin sketch of Aldo with smoke coming out of his ears.

Meanwhile, Kiana catches Aldo looking at her. Embarrassed, he picks up his soup bowl and guzzles what's left of it, pepper and all. A split second later, a green geyser of pea soup sprays across the room, propelled by a scream.

*"What did you do that for?"* he rasps.

I can't answer because I'm laughing too hard. So is Rahim. When Aldo sees the napkin sketch, he stabs it with his spoon, which snaps in half.

That gets us a caution from the lunchroom monitor, who raises the quiet alert level from green to amber on the traffic signal at the front of the cafeteria.

"You've got to tone it down, man," I manage, fighting to control my laughter. "Everything makes you fly off the handle."

"Not true!" he bellows in my face, and the traffic signal goes to red.

Now nobody's allowed to talk for the rest of lunch, and it's all Aldo's fault. Rahim and I exchange a fist-bump under the table.

Afterward, when we're walking back to room 117—I mean everybody else is walking; I'm thumping on my crutches—I can't resist rubbing a little more salt in Aldo's wounds. "Kiana was watching you the whole time," I assure him. "She probably thinks you're nuts or something."

"Did I ask you to put a pound of pepper in my soup?" he demands.

"Okay, but you don't have to get so mad about it. You're mad at me; you're mad at Rahim; you're mad at the cafeteria for changing the chicken nugget recipe; you're mad at Ribbit—"

"I'm not mad at Ribbit," he mutters.

"You said you were before."

"Yeah, well, I changed my mind."

"Fine," I agree. "Everything makes you mad *except* Ribbit." And I stop bugging him because I keep thinking about Mr. Kermit, fighting with the office to get me in the pep rally.

Back in room 117 with the rest of the class, we can't help noticing a bright green vuvuzela, bent double, sticking out of our teacher's trash can.

"If Ribbit thinks he can get rid of all those things one at a time," puts in Rahim, "he's in for a really rough Spirit Week."

"I can't understand what makes him tick," puts in Kiana. "Most of the time, he never opens his mouth, but blow a vuvuzela and he'll scream you an opera."

"They make him mad," I say, with a wink at Aldo.

"He's the Grinch!" Mateo pipes up suddenly.

"I thought he was Squidward," Parker reminds him.

Mateo shakes his head. "The Grinch—definitely. The Grinch hates Christmas because he can't stand the noise. Well, Mr. Kermit hates Spirit Week because he can't stand the vuvuzelas."

"Everybody hates something," I retort. "I don't like lima beans—am I the Grinch too?"

"It's not just what you hate; it's why you hate it," Mateo replies seriously. "Indiana Jones hates snakes because he's afraid of them. Superman hates kryptonite because it's his weakness. The Wicked Witch of the West hates water because it makes her melt. But Mr. Kermit and the Grinch are both haters for the same reason—noise."

Ribbit comes in, and the first thing he sees is all of us staring into his wastebasket at the broken vuvuzela. He seems annoyed at first, but then his expression changes to one of sympathy. "I have some bad news about Spirit Week—"

"It's okay, Mr. Kermit," Kiana interrupts. "We know you tried your best to talk the principal into letting us be a part of it."

"Let me tell you about spirit." The teacher comes alive, making eye contact with each of us as he speaks. "No one can command you to have spirit—not principals, governors, presidents, or even kings. There's no spirit switch in your brain that can be flipped on or off. Spirit isn't a week you can put on your calendar. It doesn't come from posters, or streamers, or rallies, or funny hat days. And it definitely doesn't come from making an ungodly racket with a cheap plastic instrument of torture that was invented purely for disturbing the peace!"

It's the most he's said to us all year. I can't explain it, but it feels like a kind of breakthrough—although what we're breaking through to, I have no clue.

Maybe it's this: in all my years in school, I've never heard a teacher say something that was so completely, totally honest.

# Twelve

## Parker Elias

I kick off Spirit Week by getting arrested.

I'm on my way to pick up Grams on Monday morning when this cop pulls me over because my taillight is out. The problem is this guy is new, and when I show him my provisional license, he thinks it's a fake ID. So he takes me into the police station, and by the time the desk sergeant straightens him out, I'm late for picking up Grams.

She's not waiting outside her apartment building,

but when I run upstairs and knock at the door, nobody answers. I drive around the neighborhood, and sure enough, there she is, walking along the main drag.

I pull up alongside her and lower the window. "Grams, where are you going? Get in the truck!"

She keeps on walking and never even glances in my direction. Way back when she was growing up in Israel a million years ago, her mother taught her never to get into a strange car. She forgot most of everything else—including the grandson who's supposedly her favorite person—but that stuck. I have to drive half a block ahead, park, get out, and "accidentally" run into her on the sidewalk. She recognizes me now; in fact, she's really glad to see me—but not half as glad as I am that I found her. (She could have gotten on a bus somewhere and be really lost.)

She still can't come up with my name, though. "You look skinny, kiddo. Have you been eating?"

Sigh. Why can't she just say: "You look skinny, *Parker*"?

"Hey, here's the pickup," I announce in surprise. "Hop in. I'll give you a lift."

By the time I drop her off at the senior center, I'm way late. To make things worse, I get stuck behind this giant truck in the driveway of the school. I squint at the sign on the back. At first, it looks sort of like ALIEN ROT ANT GRID, but that can't be right. Then I recognize the logo from the internet. It's Oriental Trading, that website where you can order bulk amounts of things like joke glasses and light-up necklaces and party stuff.

I honk for them to let me pass, but they're already out of the truck—two big guys. They open the back and start hauling these giant cartons onto the loading bay of the school. There's no writing on the boxes, but there's a picture, so I know exactly what's inside. Vuvuzelas for Spirit Week. Hundreds of them. If they really ordered for every class but us, a thousand.

My grip tightens on the wheel. What do I care? If SCS-8 is being left out, it makes no difference to me if they've ordered noisemakers for every man, woman, and child on the planet.

Then I think of Mr. Kermit—the way he tried to make the principal change her mind, even though he hates vuvuzelas. Man, the sound of just one drives him bananas. In all these boxes, there must be enough noise power to bring down a herd of elephants.

I pull around the truck, thumping over the curb and driving across some of the front lawn to the parking lot. (That's against the rules of my license too, but this is an emergency.) I roar into a spot, putting only a tiny scrape on the side mirror of Mrs. Oneonta's Mini Cooper. I jump out and head for the school without even using my bottle of scratch guard. By the time I hit the entrance foyer, I'm flying.

I sprint clear across the school, past the gym to room 117. What luck—the other kids are there, but Mr. Kermit hasn't arrived yet. Considering he's a teacher, he sure doesn't seem to have a problem with tardiness—his own, anyway. If they gave late slips to staff members, Ribbit would spend his whole life in detention. (Maybe that wouldn't be a bad thing for someone who loves crossword puzzles so much.)

"The vuvuzelas are coming!" I gasp.

"One if by land, or two if by sea?" Barnstorm snorts.

"This is serious," I insist. "Oriental Trading is parked out front right now, unloading them."

Kiana clues in. "Mr. Kermit's going to lose it."

"And it's going to be hard to get any rest," adds Rahim with a yawn.

"It's no fair that everybody gets them but us," Aldo complains. "I mean, I don't want a stupid vuvuzela anyway. But it's still annoying."

"Ribbit's right," says Barnstorm. "It's fine to have spirit if you really *do*—like if your team is winning the championship or something. But to have spirit because your principal tells you to—because of what *week* it is? That's just dumb."

"What does school spirit have to do with vuvuzelas anyway?" I complain. "Because they're loud? So are car accidents." I actually think about that a lot.

"Poor Mr. Kermit," Kiana adds. "This is going to be rough for him. I wish there was something we could do to make it better."

"Maybe there is," Mateo muses.

Aldo rolls his eyes. "What—we send him on vacation to the Death Star until Spirit Week is over?"

"Of course not," he dismisses this. "The Death Star is *Star Wars*. Mr. Kermit is the Grinch."

"The Grinch isn't real," Kiana explains patiently.

"But what the Grinch *did* can be real," Mateo insists. "He didn't like Christmas, so he stole it. All of it—all the Christmas stuff in Whoville. Even the Who pudding and the roast beast."

Barnstorm's eyes widen. "*Steal* the vuvuzelas? There are, like, seven of us, and I'm on crutches. How are we supposed to carry that many vuvuzelas?"

"They're in boxes," I put in. "Big ones, but I don't think they're super heavy. At least, the Oriental Trading guys are having no trouble unloading them."

"Where do we put them?" Aldo demands. "In our lockers?"

Mateo is stuck on the holiday TV special. "The Grinch loaded the Whos' Christmas stuff on a sled to dump off the top of Mount Crumpit . . ."

"Too bad there aren't any ten-thousand-foot cliffs around here—" That's when it hits me. "Guys—what about the river?" If you follow the school property straight on past the athletic fields, you'll eventually come to the banks of the Greenwich River, which divides our town in two.

Kiana shakes her head sadly. "It's just not practical. There's no way we could move giant boxes all that way."

"I'll drive them," I say suddenly. "We just have to load them into my truck." I can't quite describe how I feel. It's not that I'm so anxious to *do* it, but suddenly it just seems so *doable*. And knowing it's possible, it feels like we have to try.

Rahim looks up from his doodles. "We'll get in trouble."

No kidding. If we get caught, it's hard to imagine the school will go easy on the kids who hijacked a thousand vuvuzelas.

The answer comes from, of all people, Elaine.

"We're already in trouble," she rumbles from her spot at the back of the room. "This class *is* trouble. What can they do to us—put us in here twice?"

"Let's do it." Kiana reaches a hand into the center of our group. "For Mr. Kermit."

Barnstorm places a crutch over it. "I'll show them where they can stick their spirit."

Aldo tries to lay his hand over Kiana's, but the crutch is in the way. "Nobody tells me what to get worked up about."

"To the universe and beyond!" Mateo exclaims.

We all sign on, even Rahim, who is as close to wide awake as I've ever seen him.

"We have to hurry," I urge. "Once the custodians start unpacking those cartons, it's all over."

We head for the loading bay, taking the long way to avoid passing the faculty lounge. The last thing we need is to run into Mr. Kermit heading for room 117—not that he'd ask us where we're going.

Luckily, the halls are busy, so nobody takes much notice of us as we loop around the main foyer and backtrack to the storage rooms that connect to the loading bay.

Kiana peers around the door frame. "Uh-oh."

Following her lead, I peek into the storeroom. The

loading bay door is still open to the driveway, but the truck is gone. Just inside stand the big boxes. I count—seven of them, stacked three, two, and two. Mr. Carstairs stands next to them, the packing slip in one hand, a half-finished bagel in the other.

"Why hasn't he started unloading yet?" I murmur.

"He's probably waiting for help," Kiana whispers back. "That means the other custodians could be here soon."

Aldo curses under his breath. "How are we supposed to get the boxes with Carstairs right there?"

Mateo has an idea. "We need to create a distraction."

"What distraction?" Kiana asks.

"I can talk to him about *The Silmarillion*," Mateo volunteers. "That's the creation story for the entire mythology of *The Hobbit* and *The Lord of the Rings*. And I'll try to get him to walk away."

"That's the stupidest thing I've ever heard in my life," Barnstorm hisses. "We're going to need a better distraction than that."

"Definitely," deadpans Elaine. She rears up a heavy black boot and brings it down full force on Barnstorm's sneakered foot.

The scream could probably drown out all those

vuvuzelas put together. It causes a major freak-out in the hall. Mr. Carstairs comes running. What he sees is the school's injured sports hero, on crutches, howling in agony. The custodian gets his shoulder under Barnstorm's arm, and the two of them begin hobbling in the direction of the nurse's office.

Kiana turns accusing eyes on Elaine. "You didn't have to do that! He could have just faked it."

Aldo chortles. "Not as good as that."

We race into the loading bay.

"Oh, gross," Rahim complains.

"What's gross?" I ask.

He points. "It says it on the boxes. They're gross."

Kiana throws up her hands in exasperation. "That's not gross; that's *one gross*. It means there's a hundred and forty-four vuvuzelas in each carton."

"That makes"—Mateo does the calculation in his head—"a thousand and eight. I thought we were only getting a thousand." It really seems to bother him.

"Never mind that! I'll go for the truck!" I scramble out of the loading bay and jump the three feet down to the pavement. I sprint for the parking lot and leap into the pickup. It takes all the restraint I can muster to keep from stomping on the gas. The last thing we need is for my squealing tires to attract the attention of every adult in the school. Suddenly, my perforated muffler doesn't seem like such a great asset either. It may sound cool, but we're trying for stealth here.

I get out and scramble onto the platform to help with the loading. You know all that stuff about vuvuzelas being light? Well, that goes out the window when you're lifting a box with a hundred and forty-four of them. On the plus side, we've got Elaine, who could lift the load and the loading bay with it—and maybe the truck too.

Kiana and Mateo pile in beside me, but Aldo, Rahim, and Elaine have to jog alongside the pickup. I pull around the side of the school and then jump over the curb and start driving slowly along the grass. I glance at the rearview mirror, and see Elaine flashing me a thumbs-up. I normally try to have as little interaction with her as possible, but right now the gesture gives me heart—because I'm pretty scared at this point.

Are we crazy? Probably, but that's not the part that bothers me. My main worry is that none of this is covered by my provisional license. And if it gets revoked, who's going to pick up Grams every morning and drive her to the senior center?

# Thirteen
## Mr. Kermit

No one can stop the passage of time.

I've tried. It can't be done.

Case in point—every year in early October, Spirit Week comes along. It's like death and taxes. Actually, my 106-year-old grandfather is doing a better job at putting off death than I am at avoiding Spirit Week. There's only one word for it: *inevitable*.

At the sight of the truck from Oriental Trading, I head for the faculty lounge, fill the Toilet Bowl with coffee, and sit in a dark corner, steeling myself for what's ahead. My fellow teachers cast sympathetic glances in my general direction, but no one approaches me directly. They know there's nothing they can say. Already, those South African air horns from Hades have begun to sound in the halls. Once the mother lode is passed out, the noise will be beyond imagination.

When the cacophony starts, I resolve to close my eyes and dream of June—of early retirement, of another life beyond these walls. I'll unwind, relax, maybe travel—avoiding South Africa, of course, and any other countries where vuvuzelas are part of the local culture. That's the only thing with half a chance of getting me through this—the thought that this Spirit Week, awful as it is, will be my last.

I arrive at room 117 to find it empty. For a fleeting instant, I toy with the possibility that my dreams have come true, and every single one of the students is absent on the same day. Maybe they all gave each other mono. That would mean I could miss Spirit Week altogether!

The intercom interrupts that pleasant thought. "Mr. Kermit? It's Bonnie Fox in the nurse's office. I've got Bernard Anderson here with me."

The name doesn't ring a bell. "Bernard?"

"You know, the boy they call Barnstorm. Someone stepped on his foot, but when I asked for a name, he clammed up. I'm worried that there might be some kind of bullying involved."

I almost ask if the others are there with him, but I keep my mouth shut. On the off chance that it's true, she might send them back.

"He's already got crutches, but that seems to be unrelated," the nurse goes on. "I've iced the foot, but Bernard refuses to let me call his parents. He says he doesn't want to miss anything."

"Spirit Week," I mutter. Even students who are deliberately excluded still find something irresistible about this three-ring circus. Into the intercom, I add, "Well, thanks for letting me know. Please don't feel you have to send him back to class anytime soon. Take your time. We don't want to risk reinjury."

I break the connection. One mystery solved; six to go. Except is it really a mystery if you don't care? Just the fact that they're absent is enough for me.

At that moment, the PA system crackles to life. "Your attention, please. It's Principal Vargas." Her voice seems higher-pitched than usual, and a little shrill, like she's under stress. "Seven large cartons are missing from the loading bay. That's all the vuvu-zelas for Spirit Week. Perhaps somebody thinks this is a joke. I assure you that it isn't. This is stealing, pure and simple. If the school doesn't get its property back immediately, we'll turn the matter over to the police."

I sit down at my desk and open the paper to the crossword puzzle. Who would have believed that Spirit Week could start out on such a hopeful note? First, no students. Next, no vuvuzelas. How could it be better—Superintendent Thaddeus being abducted by aliens?

I frown. Missing students . . . missing vuvuzelas . . .

Miss Fountain bursts in from next door. At the sight of the empty desks, she exclaims, "Mr. Kermit—where are your students?"

I shoot her a coy look. "Shhh. You'll jinx it."

"But—but—" Totally flustered, she rushes across the room and yanks up the Venetian blinds.

An appalling sight meets my eyes. A pickup truck is jouncing across the schoolyard—not just any truck; *Parker's* truck. The payload is piled high with boxes. Parker is at the wheel, his face and shoulder crowded up against the driver's-side window by the rest of the missing Unteachables. Three more jog alongside the pickup.

"They hate me!" I exclaim.

"Of course they don't hate you," Miss Fountain shoots back. "Why would you say such a thing?"

"They know how much I can't stand vuvuzelas. They're cornering the market so they can torture me forever."

"Come on!" She grabs my arm and literally drags me to the nearest exit. "We've got to stop them before this becomes a police matter and the children end up in trouble!"

Out on the lawn, she runs after them, so I run too. I haven't run in fifteen years, and I'm not good at it. Six steps in, I'm out of breath. Gasping and wheezing, struggling to keep up, I reflect once again how much Emma Fountain is like her mother. In the middle of a crisis, her number one concern is that the "children" shouldn't get in trouble. Why not? Trouble was invented for juvenile delinquents who do things like this! Fiona was the same way. And her onetime fiancé used to be just as naïve—until a certain seventh grader named Jake Terranova showed me how the real world worked.

A glance over my shoulder reveals that Emma and I aren't the only ones chasing the runaway Unteachables. It looks like half the faculty is racing across the grass, running full tilt. Christina Vargas is in the lead. But wait—who's that inching ahead of her? Oh no, it's Dr. Thaddeus! The superintendent's face is bright red, and he's sweating all over his hand-tailored silk suit. Not far behind the leaders is Barnstorm, thump-swinging skillfully on his crutches. The kid really is a great athlete. He's having no problem keeping ahead of Nurse Fox and the custodial staff. Even a couple of the lunch ladies have joined the stampede.

Up ahead, the pickup stops in a spray of dirt and grass. The Unteachables set about unloading the big boxes, yanking them out of the payload.

"What's that noise?" Emma tosses over her shoulder.

I hear it too—a low, hissing rumble. The Greenwich River. The students have the boxes ripped open and lined up along the riverbank, as if they're planning to—

The truth hits me like a cannonball to the stomach, knocking the wind out of me. Or maybe it just feels that way because I have so little wind left.

They're not *stealing* the vuvuzelas; they're going to dump them!

I resolved long ago never again to waste any brain activity wondering what makes a bunch of rotten kids do what they do. But this is something that can't be ignored. Hijack a shipment of vuvuzelas only to throw them away? *Why?*

Aldo's voice reaches me from the riverbank. "It's Ribbit!"

What happens next might be the strangest part of an already bizarre episode. The Unteachables—caught red-handed in the middle of a ridiculous crime—all start *cheering*.

What choice do I have but to try to get to the bottom of this?

I charge up to the group. "Has everybody gone crazy?" I demand, panting from the long sprint. "What could possibly be the point of—" That's all the breath I have left. I double over, clutching my thighs, gasping.

"We did it, Mr. K!" Parker crows. "We got the vuvuzelas! All one thousand of them!"

"One thousand and eight!" Mateo corrects.

At this point it's just babble.

"I saw the shipment in the loading bay—"

"Elaine created a distraction on Barnstorm's foot—"

"We got the idea from the Grinch—"

I throw my arms around a carton and pick it up, nearly rupturing a disc in the process. Who knew that a box of light plastic horns could be so *heavy*?

It's a titanic struggle to get it up onto my shoulder. "We're taking these back to school right now!" I exclaim, voice strained. "Honestly, what were you kids thinking?"

Kiana regards me earnestly. "We know how you feel about Spirit Week, Mr. Kermit. We took the vuvuzelas because you hate them so much."

The bulky carton freezes on its unsteady perch on my shoulder. The thought knifes through my oxygen-starved brain. They're doing this—for *me*!

*"Kermit!"* roars an enraged Dr. Thaddeus. *"Control your students!"*

I barely hear him. The flood of emotions brings me back decades—to a time before Jake Terranova and the cheating scandal. Back when I was Emma's age, and I'd step into the classroom every morning with high hopes of shaping young minds.

The mere memory of the teacher I used to be causes my posture to straighten—and that might explain why the giant box of vuvuzelas overbalances. I cry in alarm as the carton tips over, taking me with it. As I fall, a hundred and forty-four *Go, Go, Golden Eagles* vuvuzelas drop out of the container into the water. I'm only a split second behind them, plunging headfirst into the river in a not-too-graceful reverse swan dive.

The cold water delivers a shock to my central nervous system, starting my heart beating triple time. Shivering, I break the surface just in time to see my students scrambling, tumbling, jumping, and belly flopping to my rescue. Even Barnstorm joins the mission, flinging aside his crutches and hurling himself into the drink. In the process, the kids manage to overturn the other boxes and kick most of the remainder of the shipment into the river with them.

It's a moment that's definitely not covered in teacher's college—standing with your entire class in chest-high water while a thousand and eight bobbing vuvuzelas drift off downstream. Elaine has Mateo by the collar to keep him from sailing away with the noisemakers.

Of all the miserable things that have happened to me during Spirit Week over the years, this ranks about sixth.

# Fourteen

## Dr. Thaddeus

# HIJACKED HORNS SCUTTLE SPIRIT CELEBRATION

The Greenwich Telegraph, Local News

By Martin Landsman, Staff Reporter

Greenwich Middle School's annual Spirit Week was a disappointment this year after a prank gone awry dropped a shipment of the traditional vuvuzelas into the river. Although more than half the noisemakers were eventually recovered, there was little enthusiasm at the school for blowing them. "I'm not putting my mouth on those things," one student commented. "You know, fish go to the bathroom in that water."

District officials are not revealing the names of the perpetrators of the prank, saying only that they have been "appropriately reprimanded," and that their teacher is a "veteran educator." But the *Telegraph* has learned that the teacher in question is Mr. Zachary Kermit, who is still remembered for his involvement in a 1992 cheating scandal that remains a serious black eye for the Greenwich schools. . . .

Christina Vargas finishes reading the article and slides it back across my desk. "Surely you're not still angry at Zachary Kermit for what happened twenty-seven years ago."

"Why shouldn't I be?" I ask irritably. "The whole town remembers the scandal. The fact that it came up in this story proves that."

The principal shrugs. "You know as well as I do that the real culprit was Jake Terranova. He's the one who got his hands on a stolen exam and went into business selling it to his classmates. He may have been only twelve at the time, but he was the same wheeler-dealer that he is today with his car business. All Zachary was guilty of was being fooled like everybody else. Like me, for one. And you."

I grimace. Superintendent is a powerful job, but a lonely one as well. When big decisions have to be made, there's no higher authority to appeal to. You are the law. Christina's right that in 1992, Zachary Kermit knew nothing about what the Terranova kid was up to. But when you're the big boss, you don't have the luxury of considering things like that. All that matters is *optics*. How does it *look*?

In 1992, it looked very bad. And if the mere mention of Zachary Kermit's name reopens that old wound in a newspaper article written by a reporter who probably wasn't even *born* in 1992, then the optics haven't gotten any better. An elephant never forgets; the people of Greenwich have memories that are longer still.

"The district wasn't exactly supportive when the cheating scandal was going on," the principal adds. "You can't fault Zachary for feeling abandoned. No wonder he got so burned-out."

"And what about this latest incident?" I probe.

"That wasn't Zachary's fault either," she offers. "We gave him the Unteachables. What did you expect?"

"I expect him to control seven kids. Is that so unreasonable? I knew he wasn't going to turn them into future presidents, or even into solid citizens. But to keep them from Grand Theft Vuvuzela—is that too much to ask?"

I have her there. Not even the most sympathetic principal can condone the kind of stealing, disruption, and destruction of property that transpired on Monday.

"And look what happened when he tried to stop them," I go on, pressing my advantage. "They all ended up in the river. I just got off the phone with our insurance company. They had a few choice words to say about that, let me assure you."

She sighs wanly. "I like Zachary. We started out in teaching together. He was brilliant and dedicated. What happened in 1992 destroyed his confidence. We should have stepped up to make sure he didn't blame himself. Instead, all we cared about was making sure we were covered when the newspapers got hold of the story. It ruined Zachary's career."

Another difference between principals and superintendents: principals can be nice. "He ruined his own career. He might have been a good teacher once, but he isn't anymore. I agree—we gave him the most difficult kids in the district. And he made them worse."

"He'll be out of our hair soon enough," she offers. "We both know he's planning to take early retirement."

I wince. In the education business, you don't reach the level of superintendent without knowing how to do a little homework. The health and longevity in the Kermit family are appalling. Zachary Senior celebrated his eightieth birthday by going skydiving. The grandfather just turned 106. If the youngest Mr. Kermit has the same genes, he'll be collecting a pension from the school district for more than fifty years!

"The taxpayers of Greenwich shouldn't be on the hook for a bad teacher," I tell her. "If he's fired for cause, he'll get no pension at all."

She doesn't like that. "You have no cause. Not for a few lost noisemakers and something that happened twenty-seven years ago."

"Not yet," I concede. "But I'll find cause. Zachary Kermit is untrustworthy and incompetent. I know he's your friend, but as his boss, can you really defend him?"

She doesn't answer. A principal always knows when there's deadwood on staff that needs to be cleared away.

I don't gloat. That would be unbecoming of a superintendent. But privately, I enjoy watching her squirm as she struggles to come up with an answer to that.

"I wonder," she muses finally. "When Zachary fell in the river—"

"No defense of a teacher should include a sentence that ends with 'fell in the river,'" I cut her off.

"The students didn't fall," she persists. "They jumped in because they thought they had to rescue Zachary. Remember the kids we're talking about—some of the most difficult and antisocial we've ever seen. But they're loyal to him. Why?"

Twelve hours later, as I lie in bed, trying to sleep, that *why?* is still reverberating inside my skull.

# Fifteen
## Mateo Hendrickson

The whole class gets suspended for the rest of Spirit Week. If that doesn't sound like a bad punishment, remember that your parents need to rearrange their work schedules so you're not left completely alone. I can't speak for the others, but my folks are pretty mad.

"It's no big deal," I tell my father. "Syfy is running a *Battlestar Galactica* marathon this week. That should keep me busy until at least Thursday."

Dad is like Zeus from *Percy Jackson*. No thunderbolts, but when he's in a bad mood you definitely want to stay clear of Olympus. "If you think this is a vacation, mister, you're sadly mistaken. You're going to sit in your room and reflect on how it's wrong to steal."

"It wasn't stealing," I insist. "Stealing is *The Great Train Robbery*. This is the Grinch. Better than the Grinch. The Grinch tried to steal Christmas, but he couldn't. We really did steal Spirit Week."

"You stole it from *yourselves*," he retorts. "Everyone else gets to enjoy it."

"We were already banned before we were suspended. Besides, Mr. Kermit's right. It's dumb to have spirit because it's on the calendar, or because people are blowing horns in your ear."

He frowns. "Mr. Kermit. I don't like what I'm hearing about that guy."

"Mr. Kermit's a good teacher," I argue. At least, he could be if he ever teaches anything. Look at Yoda. He may be a puppet with bad grammar, but he's also the greatest teacher in the galaxy. In fact, I might have to switch Mr. Kermit from the Grinch to Yoda, just like I'm going to have to switch Barnstorm from the Flash to Aquaman, because he's an amazing swimmer, even with a bad knee and a foot that's been stomped on by Elaine.

Come to think of it, if we're all suspended, does Mr. Kermit still have to go to school? There's nobody there for him to teach. Actually, I think he might like that. But it's possible that he's suspended too. Dr. Thaddeus seems really mad at him.

"Nah, Ribbit's not suspended," Parker tells me when I run into him on a delivery to the farmers' market. "His car's been in the parking lot all week."

"How would you know that?" I ask.

"Whenever I'm near the school on business, I look around a little."

"Business?" I echo.

"Farm business. I've got potatoes for Foodland, cantaloupes for the truck stop, and rutabagas for Local Table—Dad says they pay the most because they can't bring in produce from more than twenty miles away."

By the time we get back to school the next Monday, Spirit Week is over, and there isn't a vuvuzela in sight. Otherwise everything is the same—except for room 117. In fact, the place looks so different that, when I walk in, I actually step back into the hall to check the number on the door. No—it's 117 all right, and the other SCS-8 kids are taking their seats as usual. But we're all looking around in wonder.

There's a huge map of the world on the back wall, next to star charts from the northern and southern hemispheres. At the front, there are bulletin boards for math, science, English, and social studies. There's a rolling cart of laptop computers. There are books on the bookshelves. The empty supply closet isn't empty anymore. Through the open door we can see stacks of paper, pencils, scissors, and art supplies.

Another thing that's different: Mr. Kermit is already here. He's at the science board, pinning up a large periodic table of elements. It throws some of us because when the teacher makes his usual entrance ten minutes after the bell, that's our signal to start *ribbit*ing. Sure, there are a few *ribbits*, but they seem random and halfhearted.

Kiana speaks up. "Mr. Kermit?"

"Oh!" He turns away from the board, as if noticing us for the first time. "Good. Everybody's here. Before we get started, I want to say something about last Monday down at the river. I know you were only trying to help, so let's chalk it up to temporary insanity. And—uh—thanks. But next time—not that there will be a next time—well, please find somebody else to help."

"But, Mr. K—" Parker interjects, waving his arms to take in the transformed classroom. "What gives?"

Mr. Kermit looks uncomfortable. "Well, last week I had some spare time since all my students were—uh—absent. So I did some redecorating."

An uneasy murmur buzzes through room 117. It's hard to put my finger on it, but it comes from the fact that this "redecoration" smells an awful lot like school. It isn't a big problem for me. I'm okay with the *school* side of things. But I don't like change. And for sure, this isn't the Ribbit we're used to. Where did all this come from?

At that moment, the door is flung open, and Miss Fountain breezes in, beaming. "What do you think, everybody? Isn't it *awesome*?"

"I forgot to mention," Mr. Kermit adds. "Miss Fountain helped a lot, so we owe her a big thank-you."

Nobody utters a sound.

Our teacher shuffles uncomfortably. "Well, Miss Fountain, I'm sure you're in a rush to get back to your students—"

Miss Fountain is looking around in growing concern. "But—where is it?"

Mr. Kermit seems flustered. "Well, there wasn't much space, and—" In resignation, he walks to the storage closet and opens the door the rest of the way. On the inside is a chart with all our names in a column. At the top is written: GOODBUNNIES.

Miss Fountain's brow furrows. "This isn't going to work. It has to hang in a place where everybody can see it." She pulls the poster from the door and rehangs it on the front wall right behind the teacher's desk. "Much better."

I raise my hand. "What are Goodbunnies?"

"You are," she explains. "You're the Goodbunnies. Every time you're a helpful hare—like when you do a good deed or get a good grade—you earn one puffy-tail. When your line of puffy-tails reaches the basket of carrots, you get a reward."

"I don't like carrots," Barnstorm complains.

"It could be a treat, or maybe even a pizza party with a cake—"

"A carrot cake?" Barnstorm asks suspiciously.

"The carrots are just a symbol. Here, I'll get you started." From a baggie attached to the bottom of the poster, she removes seven Velcro-tipped cotton balls and pins one to the first slot beside each of our names.

For some reason, I feel like I've accomplished

something, even though the week has barely started.

Aldo lets out a loud raspberry. "This is stupid! What are we—five? I'm not wasting my time collecting rabbit butts."

Mr. Kermit is annoyed. "All right, smart guy. You just cost yourself one"—his face twists—"puffy-tail." He pulls off the Velcro sticker and puts it back in the bag.

"No fair," grumbles Aldo.

Miss Fountain is just about to go back to her own class when there's a knock at the door, and this new guy walks in. He's an adult, but not one of the teachers, and he looks really familiar, although I can't place where I've seen him before. Mr. Kermit knows him—that's for sure. Our teacher has gone white to the ears, like he's staring into the Great Pit of Carkoon from *Return of the Jedi*.

The newcomer says, "I don't know if you remember me, Mr. Kermit—"

As soon as I hear the voice, I recognize him.

Barnstorm beats me to the punch. "Dude—you're Jake Terranova!"

# Sixteen

## Parker Elias

Jake Terranova!

Everybody knows Jumping Jake Terranova, who will jump through hoops to get you a great deal on a new or used vehicle. The billboards are all over town (although to me, TERRANOVA MOTORS looks more like AROMAVENT ROTORS). Anyway, there's no mistaking the face. This guy's famous! What's he doing in room 117?

Mr. Kermit has an expression on his face as if he

smells something really bad. It's the way he looks when there's a vuvuzela blaring. And since the vuvuzelas are all gone, it can only mean one thing: he hates Jake Terranova's guts.

Miss Fountain steps forward. "I really should explain, Mr. Kermit. I ran into Jake—that is, Mr. Terranova—at my parents' country club. I wanted to see if he remembered me. He sold me my Prius last year."

Mr. Terranova smiles with all thirty-two teeth. "Great car. Are you in the market for a new vehicle, Mr. Kermit? Emma loves hers."

"It makes me feel good to know I'm helping the environment every time I drive," Miss Fountain says with a meaningful look over her shoulder at Ribbit.

Our teacher's eyes get so narrow that they're barely slits.

"Anyway," Miss Fountain goes on, "we got to talking, and your name came up, Mr. Kermit. I told him about that story in the *Telegraph*—"

The car dealer cuts her off. "This should come from me." He turns to Mr. Kermit. "I read the article about the vuvuzelas. They mentioned something from the past—something I was involved in."

Our teacher has his teeth clenched until his lips have practically disappeared. "Mr. Terranova used to be one of my students," he explains, his speech clipped, "some years back."

"That's not enough. They should hear the whole truth." He addresses us. "You might have heard about a cheating scandal. Well, Mr. Kermit had nothing to do with it. It was me. I can't believe the newspaper dredged up that old story."

"Don't worry about it, Mr. Terranova," I assure him. "None of us read newspapers."

"I do," Mateo puts in. "*Middle Earth Weekly*. Of course, it's more fanfic than news."

The car dealer gives him a strange look. "The point is I don't want you kids to think that Mr. Kermit did anything wrong. It was my fault. I got caught and I got suspended for it."

"No kidding," Aldo pipes up. "We just got back from being suspended. But I didn't think it would happen to a big-shot rich dude."

Barnstorm snorts a laugh. "He wasn't a big shot when he got suspended, dummy. He was a kid like us."

Aldo and Barnstorm wheel around in their seats, turning belligerent expressions on each other. But Mr. Terranova quickly steps between them. "Guys, I was in middle school once too. If you two want to throw hands, there's nothing I can do to stop it. But not here and not now."

Aldo and Barnstorm back down.

The car dealer faces Mr. Kermit again. "So I came here to apologize, which I should have done years ago. And if there's anything I can ever do to help out—you know, with the class—all you have to do is say the word."

"Thanks for your generous offer," our teacher says stiffly. "But that won't be necessary—"

"Of course we want your help!" Miss Fountain exclaims, and it's pretty obvious this was her plan all along.

Mr. Kermit's sour expression gets worse. "I'm sure Mr. Terranova wouldn't appreciate it if you and I went to his lot and tried to sell cars. And he would be just as unsuccessful trying to teach our students."

"Be reasonable," she pleads. "He's built a business. He could give a math unit on earnings versus expenses, or how to amortize a loan. He could let us tour his repair shop and maybe teach us about basic auto mechanics."

"He could let me take out a Dodge Viper for a test drive." I add, "I have a license."

Mr. Terranova doesn't answer. He's beaming at Miss Fountain, and at that moment he looks exactly like his picture on the billboards (without the flaming hoops, obviously). "It's a date," he says, and Miss Fountain's cheeks get all red, even though it isn't really hot in the classroom.

"Well, maybe," Mr. Kermit concedes. "If the curriculum allows."

"We don't have a curriculum," Mateo points out. "We just get worksheets while you do crossword puzzles."

That costs him a puffy-tail.

# Seventeen
## Mr. Kermit

The Goodbunnies chart is mocking me.

No matter where I am in the room, my eyes are drawn to the bright pink poster board with its white puffy-tails. Even at my desk—when I can't see it—I sense it behind me. Knowing it's there is almost as bad as looking at it.

As great as the temptation may be, I can't bring myself to throw it out. Emma keeps finding excuses to come over and check on it. She's frustrated that no one is earning any puffy-tails. She's determined to stick with the teaching style that worked with her kindergarten class last year. Her mother was like that—100 percent headstrong when she believed she was right. Middle schoolers won't excel for that kind of infantile reward system. And these particular middle schoolers wouldn't excel if you put ten thousand volts to the soles of their feet. The only thing that motivates them, apparently, is the prospect of dumping mass quantities of vuvuzelas into the river.

But that's another story—and a much more bizarre one. I don't like to think about that. There are some questions that should never be answered.

My new habit is to get to class before the kids. That way, I can be finished with the *New York Times* crossword puzzle by the time they arrive. Just because the school saddled me with the worst class in the district doesn't mean I have to pass that disrespect on to the students. They deserve better—some of them. One or two. And anyway, all of them jumped into the river when they thought their teacher was drowning. That says something.

I'm still not sure what.

As I spread the newspaper out, I have to push the Toilet Bowl to the edge of the desk, which sends some papers skittering to the floor. A couple of weeks ago, I would barely have noticed. But now that this place looks sort of like a real classroom, it's worth a little effort to keep things neat. If not, one of these days Emma might show up with a CLEANBUNNIES poster board, and this one will have the name ZACHARY on it.

I'm about to toss the papers when I recognize the first page. It's one of my old worksheets, accompanied by four additional pages of neat handwriting. *Kiana Roubini*, reads the name at the top. I remember her handing in something like this. And come to think of it, she's always been a little less out to lunch than the rest of them.

I scan a few lines. It's an *essay* of all things, and it seems to be pretty well written. I read on, drawn in by her compelling sentences and well-constructed arguments about mass transit. She's really enthused about the subject, and she expresses herself beautifully. What's she doing in SCS-8? This is brilliant work!

Any teacher would be delighted to receive an essay like this. Why, back when I was first starting out—

My vision clouds. That was a long time ago, when teaching was more than a job; it was a sacred mission. I was young and stupid then, and I've vowed never again to make the mistake of caring about the students. I cared about Jake Terranova once. Look where that got me.

On the other hand, it isn't Kiana's fault that Terranova went into business selling exams. It won't be breaking the promise I made to myself to give her the feedback she deserves for a fantastic piece of work.

So later, when the students arrive, I return her paper. Written across the top is: *A+ Excellent.*

She's surprised at first, then thrilled. It triggers more long-suppressed memories: well-deserved praise, pride, and satisfaction. Motivated teacher, motivated student.

Then she asks the question I expect the least: "Do I get a puffy-tail?"

Why would Goodbunnies even be on the radar screen of someone capable of writing such a top-notch essay? But I reply, "Sure, why not?"

As I attach the Velcro puffy-tail next to her name on the chart, I have the undivided attention of every soul in that classroom. If I'd taken out a sword and knighted the girl, it couldn't have been a bigger event.

Barnstorm raises a crutch. "How come she gets one of those things? What about the rest of us?"

"She wrote an essay," I explain. "If you want a

puffy-tail, you have to work for it."

"Not necessarily," Parker pipes up. "Miss Fountain says you can also get one for being a helpful hare. I drive my Grams to the senior center every day. If that's not helpful, what is?"

So he gets a puffy-tail too. That opens the flood-gates:

"I loaded the dishwasher after dinner last night!"

"I did blue face paint at the *Avatar* convention!"

"I broke scoring records in three sports!"

"I took out the garbage!"

I award puffy-tails like it's going out of style. True, most of these "accomplishments" aren't very impressive. But puffy-tails themselves are so meaningless that it would be hypocritical to raise the standard to earn them.

Rahim gets one for staying awake long enough to receive it.

Only Aldo can't come up with anything better than "On the bus today, this kid tripped over my book bag and landed in gum."

I sigh. "That doesn't sound very—uh—helpful to me."

Aldo tries again. "Well, now it's in his hair and he can't get rid of it. He looks like a doofus!"

"Dude, you could have moved your bag out of his way," Barnstorm pronounces. "That's the helpful hare way. Otherwise, you should *lose* a puffy-tail."

"He's already at zero," Mateo puts in.

"Zero is *better*!" Aldo explodes. "Because rabbit butts are stupid!"

"Easy to say when you don't have any," Barnstorm needles.

"Come on, Aldo," Kiana whispers. "You must have done something nice!"

The boy's still stumped. He sulks for the rest of the day.

Just before lunch, Emma looks in, catches sight of the poster board with so many new puffy-tails, and beams with pleasure.

When I submit the official request for a school bus, Principal Vargas regards me with deep suspicion. She's probably thinking about how many vuvuzelas you can cram into a whole bus. A lot more than a thousand, for sure.

I elaborate. "It's for a field trip."

"Field trip?" She's amazed. "For *your* kids? Where?"

"We're going to Terranova Motors." Speaking those words is even harder than I thought it would be.

"We've been invited to tour the repair shop . . ." I regurgitate Emma's reasons why this is a good idea.

"Back up, Zachary. I've known you for a long time. Why would you go anywhere near Jake Terranova?"

I sigh. "Emma found him at some country club shindig. She's a serious busybody, that one. She told him about the Spirit Week kerfuffle, and how it dredged up what happened. Now he wants to make amends."

The principal folds her arms in front of her. "And you want to give him an opportunity to clear his conscience?"

"It's not me," I admit. "It's the kids. They came alive when he walked into the room. They consider him some kind of celebrity. Listen, Christina, I know they're awful, but what we did to them is just as awful. Are we really going to keep them cooped up like prisoners until they can be the high school's headache? If there's a chance for them to have a real education, we have to take it. And if that means Jake Terranova, then so be it."

She looks at me for an uncomfortably long moment. "The last time I heard words like that, they came from a young teacher I used to work with. A teacher named Zachary Kermit."

"That person is gone forever," I assure her. "And he's

never coming back, which is a good thing because he was an idiot."

"All right, you've got your bus." The principal scribbles a signature on the requisition form and leans back in her chair, her expression sober. "One more thing, Zachary. You've probably already noticed that Dr. Thaddeus isn't exactly your biggest fan. Well, the vuvuzelas didn't do anything to change that."

"I don't lose sleep over what *he* thinks." That's mostly because I have such terrible insomnia that there isn't much sleep for me to lose. But I don't mention that to Christina.

"You didn't hear this from me," she persists, "but I think he's going to try to go after your early retirement."

I shrug. "He's done it already. I know why I got saddled with the Unteachables. He wants me to quit. He'll see his own ears first."

"There's another way," she reminds me grimly. "One wrong step and he'll fire you. Don't give him cause. I'll protect you as much as I can, but I'm not the superintendent. He is. And never underestimate how much power that gives him."

I nod, take the bus authorization, and get out of

there. It's the cheating scandal, still haunting me after all these years. Thaddeus will never forgive me for it.

I thought Jake Terranova was back. Correction: he never left.

# Eighteen

## Kiana Roubini

**TOP 4 REASONS WHY MY HALF BROTHER, CHAUNCEY, IS LIKE VLADIMIR:**

1. The smell. Dirty diapers and baby puke. Enough said. Vladimir's terrarium after the weekend is no perfume factory either.
2. The noise. Chauncey's howling has the edge in volume, but Vladimir's high-pitched squeaks are even more piercing. It goes

without saying that both of them are spoiled by too much attention. That's Stepmonster's fault in Chauncey's case. For Vladimir, it's Miss Fountain's seventh graders, and, lately, us. When he wants somebody to feed him a dead cricket—which is all the time—the cheeping and chirping are at a frequency that feel like a miniature blender at the center of your brain.

3. The teeth. They both have zero. Okay, Vladimir probably has more than that, but you don't know they're there until he nips you. And to be fair, Chauncey does have a couple of chompers breaking through, bottom front. It's pretty cute, actually.

4. The time-suck. That's the biggest similarity between them. Dealing with Chauncey is a twenty-five-hour-per-day job, mostly for Stepmonster, but also for Dad and me. If you leave him alone for ten seconds, he'll find a way to stick his drool-covered finger into an electric outlet, light himself on fire, and roll down at least one flight of stairs. Vladimir is every bit as impossible to ignore. When he starts squeaking, you go running. And he's

not satisfied with just anybody. These days, the attention he craves is from Aldo. Leave it to Vladimir to love the least lovable person in the whole school, except maybe Elaine. Maybe it's the red hair. It's hard to ignore.

Anyway, I shouldn't really complain that Stepmonster is so distracted. If it wasn't for Chauncey, she might call up the school to ask how I'm doing and get told, "Kiana who?" The last thing I need is to get put in regular classes and have to break in eight new teachers, just when I'm starting to get the hang of Mr. Kermit.

Now that Ribbit's doing real teaching, I don't even have to make things up when Dad and Stepmonster ask, "How's school?" I have something to tell them. There are things going on in room 117—things beyond worksheets and crossword puzzles.

"Hang on a sec. Back up." My father stops me at dinner. "What are these puffy-tails you keep talking about? Some kind of science unit?"

"Right," I stammer. "Animal anatomy."

"If you're going to be dissecting some poor little bunny, I don't want to hear about it," Stepmonster puts in, shoveling strained bananas into Chauncey's waiting mouth.

"And we're going on that field trip tomorrow, remember?" I move on quickly.

"To a rabbit laboratory?" Dad asks.

"No, this is different."

We're going to Terranova Motors as Jake Terranova's personal guests. I don't know what we're supposed to learn there, but the class is actually pretty psyched about it. One of the downsides of being in SCS-8—besides the obvious—is that you're stuck in the same room all day. So the change of scenery will do us good.

Our two chaperones are Mr. Kermit and Miss Fountain. Mr. Kermit has no choice, but it's really nice of Miss Fountain to volunteer, since her own classes have to have a sub today. As it turns out, they get Mrs. Landsman—aka Dawn of the Dead. Poor Vladimir. If he squeaks too loud, she'll probably gut him with a protractor and barbecue him on a rotating spit in the home and careers room.

The bus is just a minibus, and it's pretty uncomfortable with the whole class packed into one side and Elaine all by herself on the other. Aldo is getting mad because Barnstorm keeps thumping the back of his seat with one of the crutches. It doesn't bother Rahim, though. He falls asleep as soon as we make the right turn out of the school driveway. Mateo stands in the aisle, knees bent, working on his balance, just like the Silver Surfer from *Spider-Man*.

Miss Fountain seems pretty uncomfortable with the bad behavior—and especially the fact that Mr. Kermit isn't saying anything. So she tries to change the subject by talking about how SCS-8 should participate in the district science fair. She's always coming up with suggestions for our class, like the Goodbunnies thing, or inviting us for Circle Time or to help out with Vladimir.

Sometimes, Mr. Kermit lets her push him around a little, but not today. "No," he says simply. I think this field trip has put him in a bad mood. It's pretty obvious that Jake Terranova isn't his favorite person.

"But it's a fantastic competition," Miss Fountain persists. "Teams enter from every school in the district. There are prizes. And the first-place winners get an extra ten percent added to their grades on the state science assessment. It's a win-win."

"Not for us," Mr. Kermit replies firmly.

His expression says it all: *Do these really look like the kind of kids who will come in first place at anything?*

It bugs me a little. Not that I'm dying to get mixed

up in any science fair, me being a short-timer. But I'm used to Mr. Kermit sticking up for us, not writing us off. Maybe it's part of his bad mood.

The other kids talk about Jake Terranova like he's some kind of superstar. As we pull up to Terranova Motors, I finally understand why. It has to be the biggest car dealership I've ever seen—and that includes LA, where everything is kind of supersized. Mr. Kermit's ex-student owns all this? That's pretty cool—especially when Mr. Terranova himself comes out to welcome us.

"Hey, guys! Glad you could make it! Come on inside!" Like we're longtime friends, not random middle schoolers getting our moment with the big boss.

We tour the showroom first, which, I have to admit, is pretty fun. All the vehicles are shiny, new, and top-of-the-line. We try out every seat in every car—front, back, and third row—and even climb into the payloads of the pickups. For the first time since blundering into SCS-8, I feel like I could be with any class of kids in the country, not Greenwich Middle School's dreaded Unteachables. Ribbit sees it too—his bloodshot eyes are half-open, instead of the usual 25 percent. Or maybe he's just on the alert because Mr. Terranova is here, and this is enemy territory.

Miss Fountain, the Prius driver, is looking disapprovingly at the giant SUVs and light trucks that dominate the showroom when Mr. Terranova walks up to her.

I'm wondering if she's going to lecture him on the environment. Instead, she says, "This is a wonderful thing you're doing. I don't know if you can tell, but some of these kids have—special issues."

"You think?" His grin is irresistible. "My floor manager just pulled a sleeper out of the trunk of that Cadillac."

"That's Rahim," Miss Fountain explains. "He doesn't get enough sleep at home. But he's a talented artist, sensitive and observant. They've got their quirks. They're good kids, though. Okay, maybe *good* is too strong a word—"

"Gotcha." He's watching Barnstorm poking tires with his crutches.

"Hey, Mr. Terranova." Parker approaches. "I want to take the red Mustang out for a test drive."

"Right. Very funny, kid."

"No, really. I have a license." Parker digs a mangled ID out of the pocket of his jeans.

"It's a provisional license, Parker," Miss Fountain reminds him gently.

"This is a hundred percent farm business," Parker promises. "I just remembered I've got to swing home and pick up a load of turnips for the Safeway."

Looking for a lifeline, she calls out, "Mr. Kermit, I think it's time for lunch!"

It's hard to get a handle on what Ribbit thinks of all this. On one hand, it's obvious that he can't stand his former student because of what happened in the past. On the other, that must have been forever ago. Mr. Terranova was a seventh grader, even younger than we are. He's an adult now, running a big business, and he's trying to make amends. Why can't Mr. Kermit see that?

We brought bag lunches, but Mr. Terranova ordered pizza for everybody in the dealership dining room. Only Ribbit turns him down—like anything from his old nemesis would turn to poison as soon as it enters his mouth.

The employees are really friendly, and we get to ask them questions. I want to know about fuel-efficiency standards. Barnstorm wants to know: "When you sell a car, do you get to keep the money?" Aldo asks the lease specialist, "How long did it take to grow that mustache?"

Elaine gets into the cookie platter set aside for

customer appreciation week.

After lunch, we tour the service department. That's where the field trip starts to get really good. Motor vehicles are such a huge part of life, especially in a place like LA, where you have to drive pretty much everywhere. People take it for granted that their cars will work, like they're powered by some kind of magic. How often do we ever take a peek under the hood at the machinery that makes it happen?

Mr. Terranova leads us onto a raised catwalk, and we can look down on at least a dozen vehicles on lifts in various stages of being taken apart and put back together again. The noise is a cacophony of revving engines, pneumatic tools, and the clang of metal on metal. The smell is a mix of oil and grease, with a little bit of exhaust, whatever the ventilation fans miss. Yet there's almost a kind of grace to it, and a rhythm that's hard to resist. It feels *productive*, like necessary work is being done.

Parker is practically drooling, and even Aldo is leaning over the railing, fascinated. It's the first time I've ever seen him interested in something, and he looks older and more mature. Mateo is babbling about how the shop reminds him of the engine room of the USS *Enterprise* on *Star Trek*. Rahim is sketching furiously on a napkin from the lunchroom. Elaine is watching in rapt attention while double-fisting stolen cookies from her jacket pockets.

Suddenly, she clutches the rail in distress. For a second, I wonder if she's trying to hype her reputation by ripping it free from the catwalk. But no—her cheeks are pink, her eyes terrified. Sharp staccato choking sounds reach me over the clamor of the shop. Mr. Kermit pounds her on the back, but to no avail.

I run up behind Elaine and reach around her to perform the Heimlich maneuver, positioning my hands below the rib cage, like they told us in lifesaving class back in California. Once . . . twice. No good. Three times—

"Heads up!" bellows a wild voice.

I glance over my shoulder just in time to see a crutch hurtling toward me in a home run swing. I drop to the metal floor of the catwalk a split second before the wooden shaft would have taken my head off. It slams across Elaine's broad back and—with a thud that momentarily drowns out the noisy shop—splits in two.

Everybody waits for her to crumple to the catwalk, unconscious, but that's not what happens. Elaine doesn't even flinch. Instead, a chunk of cookie comes flying out of her mouth. It sails over the rail and drops into the half-disassembled motor of a vintage Corvette.

The mechanics look up in horror.

"What was that?" Mr. Terranova asks urgently.

I confirm that Elaine is no longer choking. "She's okay."

The car dealer looks at me like I'm totally missing the point. "But what did she spit in the engine?"

Elaine smacks her lips. "I think it was a gingersnap."

The word is like a panic alarm to Jake. "Guys!" he calls down to his team. "I want that engine taken apart and every piece wiped clean! *Now!*"

I'm mystified. "What's so bad about a gingersnap?"

"Sugar!" he exclaims in agony. "It's the last thing you want in a car engine. It dissolves in the gas and ends up everywhere. If word gets around that I sold a car with a sugared tank, I'm *finished* in this business."

Mr. Kermit is beaming from ear to ear. It's the first time we've ever seen him so happy, and what did it take? Problems for Jake Terranova. I actually feel a little guilty. I saw Elaine pocketing those cookies, and kept my mouth shut. I may be a short-timer, but you don't have to be at our school very long to know that Elaine rhymes with pain.

The field trip breaks up soon after that. Mr. Terranova is focused on the Corvette, so he's not playing host anymore. Plus, Barnstorm is complaining about his mobility with only one crutch.

"Then you shouldn't have busted the other one over Elaine's head," Aldo tells him.

"It was her back, not her head," Barnstorm retorts. "I saved her life, man. She'd better remember that while deciding who her next victim's going to be."

"You just cost yourself a puffy-tail, buster," Mr. Kermit snaps.

Barnstorm is bitter. "No fair! I save a life and I'm out a crutch *and* a puffy-tail? What kind of justice is that?"

"He should *earn* a puffy-tail for helping and lose it for being mean," Parker puts in. "At least then he breaks even."

"We should all get a puffy-tail except Elaine," Aldo reasons truculently. "You know, for *not* barfing a cookie into that Corvette." This seems to be his idea of fairness.

Elaine tosses a mild glance in Aldo's direction, and he decides to stand on the other side of a tall cargo van.

It's too bad that such a great field trip has to end on

a down note. But by then the minibus is waiting outside, so there's nothing to do but get on it.

Halfway back to school, Miss Fountain gets a call on her cellphone. It's the dealership. There's a middle school boy asleep on the couch in the showroom.

Mr. Kermit does a head count. "It's Rahim," he reports. "We have to go back and get him." And we turn around.

"Wait." I frown at Miss Fountain. "How come they called *you*? I mean, why does Jake Terranova have your phone number?"

She blushes the color of Chauncey's diaper rash.

# Nineteen

## Parker Elias

Grams has a lot of life experience, being super old and all that. For example, she tells me that when she was first dating my grandfather back in Israel, there was this other girl who was trying to steal him away while Grams was doing her military service in Haifa. So Grams challenged this girl to an arm-wrestling match, and the prize was Grandpa.

I peer over at her in the passenger seat of the pickup. "What if you lost?"

"I was loading supply trucks, kiddo. I was strong as an ox."

As much as I love Grams, I'm not so sure I believe the story. The last time she explained how she got rid of the girl who moved in on Grandpa, she said she backed over her Vespa with a jeep. Grams tells the same stories because she doesn't remember telling them last time and the time before that. Some people might find that annoying; to me it just means that we've always got something new and interesting to talk about while I'm driving her around. I just wish she could remember my name.

The reason the subject comes up—dating and boy-friends, I mean—is that there's a rumor that Miss Fountain and Jake Terranova are going out. Our class thinks this because Jake has kind of adopted SCS-8. Jake—that's what he told us to call him. Even the employees at the dealership call him Mr. Terranova, but to us, he's Jake. Except Ribbit. He always uses *Mr.* when he talks to Jake, which is almost never. (Jake may be hitting it off with Miss Fountain, but he isn't getting very far with Mr. Kermit.)

Here's how it usually goes down. Jake shows up in room 117 to invite us to Terranova Motors so the mechanics can show us how windshield wipers work, or how a battery supplies power to the starter. He has to come in person because Mr. Kermit's phone is so old that it would probably explode if it ever received a text. Meanwhile, Miss Fountain randomly walks in from 115—"Oh, what a surprise. Mr. Terranova's here." She calls him Mr. Terranova too. (We're not fooled. He calls her Emma.)

From there, something always happens to connect our two classes. Maybe Vladimir starts squeaking because he hears Aldo's voice, and won't shut up until Aldo goes over there. Or the seventh graders are just about to have Circle Time, and we get in on that. Jake loves Circle Time, and whenever it's his turn to compliment someone, he always picks Miss Fountain.

Mateo is confused. "I thought Jake chose us because he wants to make up for the cheating scandal, not because of Miss Fountain."

"That's just his excuse," Barnstorm puts in wisely.

"Do you think it's the car?" I muse. Jake rolls this really snazzy Porsche convertible that's got to be a lot of fun to drive.

"Of course it's not the car," Kiana retorts angrily. "Miss Fountain isn't that kind of person. She wants a *relationship*."

I don't understand how Kiana can know something

like that. But whatever the reason, life is definitely better since Jake started hanging around. Everybody loves him—even Aldo, and Aldo hates everybody. Jake's more like another kid than an adult—but a kid who has a dream life, with tons of money and no adults telling him what to do. He talks to me about cars, to Barnstorm about sports, and to Mateo about *Game of Thrones*. He talks to Elaine—I guess car dealers don't worry about being head-butted down stairs or tossed into garbage dumpsters. He talks to Kiana about practically everything. He asks Rahim's opinion on the art for new ads for Terranova Motors, and Rahim never so much as yawns when he's around.

The only person Jake can't schmooze is Mr. Kermit. Our teacher isn't quite mean to him. Most of the time, he just ignores Jake the way he used to ignore us. When Mr. Kermit's old car breaks down, he has it towed all the way across town, even though Jake offers to fix it for free. Ribbit would rather pay a lot of money than accept a favor from his old enemy.

Whatever the reason Jake has started hanging around, the trips to Terranova Motors are amazing. At first, the service staff aren't too thrilled to see Elaine because of what happened that time with the cookie.

But then the compressor for the pneumatic system conks out, and Elaine's the only one who can loosen a stripped bolt using a hand wrench.

All the mechanics stop what they're doing and applaud.

"Kid, that was something!" the service chief exclaims admiringly. "If the lift system loses power, can we count on you to pick up cars on your shoulders?"

It's the first time I've ever seen Elaine blush. I'll bet the kid she head-butted down the stairs wouldn't think it's so funny that an eighth-grade girl is stronger than a shop full of adult mechanics.

At first, the mechanics just talk a lot and show us stuff, but pretty soon we're doing real work. Jake guides my hand as I fit a new hose into the radiator of a Jeep Cherokee. As I set the ring to seal the connection, it just feels right. Somehow, I *know* that hose isn't going to leak.

The boss reaches in and tests my handiwork. "Perfect. Not so tight that the rubber might split. Nice job, Parker."

It's weird. I open a book, and the letters are all jumbled together into Unbreakable Code. But I look at a car engine and it all makes sense—even if the tires still say READY GOO. (That's supposed to be GOOD-YEAR.)

Mr. Kermit is watching me, and he's almost smiling. I think I can count on a puffy-tail being added to my line of the chart today.

Terranova Motors isn't the only place we're doing real work. It's happening in room 117 too. Mr. Kermit is teaching stuff—math, science, English. We have our first test of the year—social studies—and Mr. Kermit even grades it.

When we get to class the next day, our papers are facedown on our desks.

Aldo flips his over. "D? Ribbit never gave tests before, and now he's throwing Ds around?"

Barnstorm laughs in his face. "It isn't Ribbit's fault you're stupid." He examines his own paper. The word *INCOMPLETE* is written across the top.

"What?!" he complains.

"At least I *got* a grade," Aldo tells him.

"I miss the old Ribbit," Barnstorm complains.

"Yeah," Aldo agrees. "This is way too much like education."

I get an incomplete too—mostly because I finished only seven of the twenty questions. But—I blink—seven check marks parade down the page. Which means whatever I did I aced! I still got an incomplete—but not incomplete-dumb, just incomplete-*slow*.

It stinks to fail, whatever the reason. But I disagree with Aldo and Barnstorm that our class was better before. We'll be in high school next year. Will they have an SCS-9 for us? Followed by SCS-10, SCS-11, and SCS-12? And then what? Sooner or later, something has to change. It might as well start now.

As I take my seat, I catch a glimpse of the test paper on Elaine's desk. I shake my head. I must be reading it wrong. That's what I do. On the other hand, how do you scramble a single letter?

If I didn't know better, I'd swear Elaine (rhymes with pain) just pulled an A.

# Twenty

## Jake Terranova

As I cruise along River Street with the top down, the red brick of Greenwich Middle School heaves into view. That place used to be a bad memory. I was never much of a student, but middle school was a really rough time. I was lucky to get away with a suspension over the cheating thing. If my dad hadn't belonged to the same college fraternity as a couple of school board members, I probably would have been expelled. It was that close.

Now, though, Greenwich Middle School means Emma. She's the best thing that's ever happened to me. Just the thought that she's somewhere inside the building puts a smile on my face.

The smile disappears when I recognize the figure standing at the entrance to the driveway, glancing impatiently at his watch. Mr. Kermit, my old teacher. The man who has every reason to drink from the Haterade where I'm concerned.

Back in seventh grade, I was so happy not to be expelled that there wasn't another thought in my head. It never crossed my mind that the episode might cause problems for my teacher. Why would it? Mr. Kermit was completely innocent. Who knew that better than the guy who was completely guilty?

But that's only the half of it. According to Emma, Mr. Kermit's life crashed after that. His reputation was shot. His engagement to Emma's mom fell apart. And he got totally burned-out professionally.

Honestly, I had no clue until Emma showed me the article about the vuvuzelas. The fact that the scandal still sticks to Mr. Kermit after all these years is nuts. Not that I ever had the power to change anything. I was a middle school kid in big trouble. I followed my parents' instructions to the letter—basically, shut up and keep your nose clean.

Now that I know the extent of it, I'd do *anything* to make things right. The problem is it's too late. Sure, Mr. Kermit is letting me help with his class of Unteachables. And I'm getting along great with the kids. But as for the teacher himself, no dice.

I check the clock on my Porsche's high-tech dashboard. It's only two p.m. Why isn't Mr. Kermit in school?

I pull alongside him and wave. Mr. Kermit scowls at me with what Mateo calls the Squidward-Grinch face. That kid's pretty weird, but he's usually spot-on. He's nicknamed me Han Solo because both of us are "lovable scoundrels." Maybe I walked away from the cheating scandal with a slap on the wrist, but lately it's come back to haunt me in all sorts of ways.

"Everything okay, Mr. Kermit?" I ask.

"My taxi is late."

Right. His "car" is in the shop. I volunteered to fix it no charge, but he wasn't having any of that. To say he's stubborn as a mule is an insult to mules.

"Hop in," I invite. "I'll give you a ride wherever you need to go."

"No, thanks," he replies formally. "I've been waiting

forty minutes for this taxi. It'll be here any second."

"It's not coming," I persist. "Did you try Uber?"

He looks blank. I remember that Mr. Kermit has a flip phone that's probably as old as his car. There are smart phones and dumb phones. His is a rock.

I unlock the passenger door. "Mr. Kermit—please. Let me give you a lift."

When he reluctantly gets in and announces his destination, I nearly choke. He's going to pick up his car—from Kingston's Auto Works.

"Are you serious? You took your car fifteen miles out of town just to avoid my offer to fix it for free?"

The response is a heavy dose of the Squidward-Grinch face. "I don't want to owe you anything."

"You *wouldn't* owe me anything!" I'm practically whining. "I would have been happy to do it."

He's sarcastic. "Well, so long as *you're* happy."

"That's not what I mean and you know it. I enjoy doing favors for friends"—Mr. Kermit doesn't like that, so I adjust my word choice—"for people I know. You used to be my teacher."

"I remember."

This is it—my chance to clear the air and apologize. But as soon as the thought pops into my head, I know he won't let me. Better to shut up about it. Maybe, as the two of us spend more time together, I'll get another chance.

And maybe the moon will fall out of the sky.

When the Porsche reaches Kingston's Auto Works, Mr. Kermit takes out his wallet and tries to pay me for the gas. When I won't accept it, he stuffs a twenty-dollar bill into the glove compartment and gets out, not bothering to say thank you.

I get out too, and receive a generous helping of Squidward-Grinch face.

"I can handle it from here," he assures me.

"I'm going in with you," I insist. "I don't want you to get ripped off. These guys are all crooks."

"Including you?" Mr. Kermit inquires innocently.

I run a totally honest shop, but still I feel my cheeks flush. "An old clunker like yours—the parts probably have to come from the third world. Who knows what they'll try to charge you for them."

It must make an impression, because Mr. Kermit actually allows me to follow him inside.

The place is a dump. You could probably catch plague just standing there breathing the air.

The mechanic behind the counter instantly recognizes me. "Hey, you're Jake Terranova. What are you doing here?"

"My *very good friend* is picking up his car," I reply pointedly. "I want to make sure he gets a fair deal."

"We barely know each other." Mr. Kermit sets the record straight.

The mechanic picks up a clipboard. "Which car?"

"The Coco Nerd," the teacher tells him.

"The *what?*"

Mr. Kermit flushes. "It's a Chrysler Concorde—1992. One of my students calls it that. He's—different."

I snap my fingers. "Parker, right? What's up with that kid? He's got a lot of mechanical ability. But ask him to read the name off a part, and it comes out pure gobbledygook."

"It's not gobbledygook," he says, insulted on Parker's behalf. "The boy has a perception problem. He sees all the letters, but his mind rearranges them—*Concorde* to *Coco Nerd*."

"Like an anagram," the mechanic butts in. "You should meet my boss—he's an anagram maniac. You look at a word, and to you it's just a jumble, but he can pick it out in a heartbeat."

Poor Parker. The kid's got real potential, but how's

he ever going to pass an engineering exam if he can't read the questions? "All right, where's the car?"

"Car's not ready," the mechanic tells us. "There's a part coming from the Bahamas, and it's held up in customs."

Instead of getting mad, Mr. Kermit acts like he's in a completely different world. "Anagrams," he repeats slowly. He grabs my arm. "Let's go."

"You have to stick up for yourself," I say sternly. I turn to the mechanic. "Is this what you call service? If I ran my shop this way, I'd be out of business in a week. How's the part coming from the Bahamas—by manatee?"

"It doesn't matter," Mr. Kermit insists. "Take me to the bookstore."

"The *bookstore*? You don't need books; you need *wheels*!"

Back in the Porsche, he explains what all this is about. "Parker's mind turns text into anagrams."

"Yeah? So?"

"So anagrams are something you can get good at, like any other puzzle."

I stare at him. "Solving anagrams can teach you to read?"

Mr. Kermit shakes his head. "Of course not. Parker

needs a reading specialist. If I was half a teacher, I would have gotten him one weeks ago."

I'm confused. "So where do the anagrams fit in?"

"The kid's reading has been a disaster for so long that he looks at it like it's magic—something he'll never be able to master. But solving anagrams will show him it can be done. So when I get him the help he needs, he'll believe it can work."

"*Can* you get him the help he needs?" I ask.

"The district has reading specialists," he explains. "Nobody sends them to SCS-8 because they consider my students a lost cause. That ends now." He glares at me. "The bookstore!"

I step on the gas and the Porsche surges forward. It's amazing how Mr. Kermit's whole face changes when he's talking about the kids in his class. He becomes a totally different person—younger, more alive. He's the teacher I remember from all those years ago.

At the bookstore, he's a whirlwind, stacking up an armload of anagram puzzle books tall enough for him to hold in place with his chin. By this time, school is out, so he demands to be taken to Parker's *house*.

"Can't you just wait to see him tomorrow morning?"

"I want to strike while the iron is hot."

The Elias family lives just outside the Greenwich

city limits on a small farm that was designed to keep sports cars out. The long "driveway" is really just a pair of ruts worn into the unpaved ground by vehicles much higher and wider than the Porsche. I can actually feel the weeds brushing the low undercarriage as we jounce along. Eventually, we come to a low wood-frame home next to a shed amid fields of tall corn.

No sign of life from the house. I cut the engine. "Should I honk?"

"Let's give it a while," Mr. Kermit decides.

After about fifteen minutes, Parker comes roaring up the drive, his famous grandmother in the passenger seat of the pickup. I know a moment of agony as the kid pulls far too close behind the parked convertible.

Parker is pretty bewildered to see his teacher rushing across the front lawn toting a pile of books he can barely see over.

The grandmother spies me standing by my car. "I know you," she calls. "You're Jumping Jake Terranova."

"That's right, ma'am. Pleased to meet you."

She beams. "I see you on television. You'll jump through hoops to provide fast relief from painful athlete's foot fungus."

"That's not me," I tell her. "I get you a great deal on a new or used vehicle."

She looks at me like I'm feeble-minded. "Why would I need that? I've got my grandson to drive me around."

Mr. Kermit is having an animated conversation with Parker, holding up anagram books and talking a blue streak. They're well into it when a small tractor chugs out of the field and an older, taller version of Parker hops off and joins the group. Parker's dad is surprised that a teacher would make house calls, but as Mr. Kermit explains his plan, the man looks impressed and smiles with appreciation.

The contrast isn't lost on me—Mr. Elias's gratitude for a teacher who's willing to move heaven and earth to help a student, versus my folks all those years ago. They rescued their son—and I'm thankful. But in the process, they hung the teacher out to dry.

Mr. Kermit deserved better. I hope someday I'll get the chance to make it up to him.

# Twenty-One
## Kiana Roubini

**N**O BIKINI AURA.

That has nothing to do with bathing suits. It's an anagram of my name.

Mr. Kermit has me working with Parker on anagrams to improve his reading. Parker's getting pretty good, but for me, it's just fun. It's amazing the stuff you can come up with. For example, ZACHARY KERMIT can be scrambled into CRAZY TRAM HIKE, or ALDO BRAFF into FOLD A BARF.

Even Aldo laughs at that one, and he doesn't strike me as someone with a great sense of humor—especially about himself. He looks pretty different when he smiles—like his face is going along with all that red hair instead of fighting against it.

Or maybe Aldo decides to be mellow because he doesn't have a lot of choice. His reading partner is Elaine. It's one thing to kick a locker. A locker can't head-butt you down a flight of stairs, or any other of Elaine's Greatest Hits, like chucking a fire extinguisher at your face, or giving you a new ear piercing with a fishhook.

To everybody's surprise, Elaine turns out to be kind of a serious student, which nobody noticed before, since they were too busy being terrified of her. Mr. Kermit assigns them *Where the Red Fern Grows*, and Elaine is totally into it. So Aldo has to read it too, even though he claims the last book he finished was *Hop on Pop*.

The other reading group is Barnstorm, Mateo, and Rahim. This works because Mateo never shuts up, which keeps Rahim from falling asleep. Actually, Rahim is more awake lately anyway. Mr. Kermit talked to his stepdad, who agreed to move his rock band's nighttime rehearsals to an "alternate venue."

Guess where—an empty storage garage at Terranova Motors.

Sometimes, I join those guys because Parker goes to a reading specialist three days a week. That makes four of us, but it's usually just three, because Rahim isn't around as much these days. Mr. Kermit got him accepted as a part-time art student at the community college on the other side of the river. Since he draws all the time anyway, it makes sense to send him somewhere that's a good thing. It's complicated, but it works. On any given day, Barnstorm might have three partners, or two, or just one. It doesn't make that much difference, because the only thing he really cares about is puffy-tails.

Like any athlete, Barnstorm's competitive. But since he's sidelined from sports, all that competitive energy gets channeled into Goodbunnies. His parade of puffy-tails stretches past the basket of carrots, off the poster, and two-thirds of the way across the wall. He's miles ahead of me in second place. Mostly, that's because he won't cash them in. He's too greedy.

Whenever my line of puffy-tails reaches the carrots, I redeem them for a reward. Our class has already had two pizza parties, thanks to me. Plus, I lent Aldo a bunch so he could pay off the penalties for some late homework assignments. That was Mr. Kermit's idea. He's using puffy-tails to teach us how an economy works. We're free to trade them, spend them, sell them, or lend them—but the lenders have to charge interest. Aldo owes me 10 percent every week, and he's sinking deeper and deeper into debt.

"You're a sucker," Barnstorm tells me. "He's never going to pay you back. It's puffy-tails down a sink-hole."

"He is so," I defend Aldo. "And with interest."

"Using what?" Barnstorm retorts. "He's never earned a single puffy-tail."

Aldo leaps up. "I have too! I just spend mine on fines and stuff."

"Sit," Elaine rumbles, and Aldo plunks back down onto his chair.

Barnstorm won't let it go. "Name one thing you ever did for a puffy-tail."

Aldo thinks hard. "I—I changed the bulb in the projector."

"No, that was Rahim," Mateo puts in.

In frustration, Aldo runs his hands through his red hair, which makes it even messier. "Big deal. Who cares about a bunch of rabbit butts?"

I glare at Barnstorm. "I have faith in Aldo."

"Oh yeah?" he shoots back. "Why?"

It's a good question. Why would I put my trust in a bad-tempered redhead and a straight-D student? Well, part of it is probably because I don't care that much about puffy-tails to begin with. But I think the other part might be Vladimir. Eight classes a day make their way through room 115, and that lizard doesn't squeak his head off for any of them. He loves Aldo—only Aldo. And aren't animals supposed to have instincts about people who are good at heart?

I turn on Barnstorm. "At least Aldo's not a tight-fisted cheapskate like you. When the year's over and we're in high school, all those puffy-tails will be worthless."

"You can't take it with you," Elaine adds philosophically.

Barnstorm is smug. "At least I'll be rich."

"You're a Ferengi," Mateo tells him. "That's a race of aliens from *Star Trek*. They worship money and profit above all things."

"Settle down," Mr. Kermit says mildly. "We're free to spend—or not spend—our puffy-tails however we choose. That's how a market economy works."

As we settle back to work, I can't help thinking about what I said to Barnstorm: *When the year's over and we're in high school . . .*

I'm not going to be in high school with these kids. I'll be gone before the end of the semester. How many times can Mom's movie get struck by lightning?

But at the moment the words were coming out of my mouth, I meant them. I actually saw myself finishing out the year in this class I don't belong in, in this school I don't really go to. And in this town where my only connection is the fact that my parents grew up here.

Oh man, I've got to get back to LA—and fast.

# Twenty-Two

## Mrs. Vargas

In all my years in education, the greatest teacher I've ever worked with was a young man named Zachary Kermit. Oh, sure, we were all dedicated back then—fresh out of college and convinced we were destined to change the world one student at a time. Zachary was different. All teachers dream of changing lives; he really changed them. The kids had no way of knowing it, but being placed in Mr. Kermit's class was like winning the lottery. It actually got to the point where I'd look out over my own group and feel a little sorry for them because there was a much better teacher just down the hall.

That was before the Terranova incident turned him into a zombie. He went from best to worst. If I were doing my job, I'd have fired him long ago, because heaven knows he wasn't doing *his* job. Maybe I didn't see things clearly enough because he was a friend. Or maybe I was waiting for the teacher he once was to reappear. But after twenty-seven years, even I had to know that the old Zachary Kermit was gone forever.

Well, guess what: he's back. And it took the worst group of kids in the whole district to make it happen.

That's what brings me to the district offices this afternoon. The first semester progress reports are out, and I can't wait to share the big news with Dr. Thaddeus.

When it's my turn, I don't even say hello to my boss. I just march in and place the seven pages on the blotter in front of him.

"What are these?" he asks.

"Progress reports from SCS-8," I tell him. "Prepare to be amazed."

He sifts through the papers, giving a cursory scan to

each. "You're right," he says finally. "I am amazed—that an experienced administrator like yourself would be fooled so easily."

I'm shocked. "Fooled? Look at those results. Okay, they're just brief summaries, but last year these kids were all floundering. This is miraculous."

"It would be," he concedes, "if it was real."

"Why wouldn't it be real? Zachary Kermit is a fantastic teacher. Oh, sure, he was in a funk for a while—"

"I'd hardly describe twenty-seven years as a 'while,'" the superintendent puts in drily.

"But these kids and their needs have brought him back," I persist. "It's wonderful."

"It's phony," he retorts.

"Zachary would never falsify student reports."

"To keep his job long enough to finish out the year he would," he tells her. "Your Mr. Kermit has figured out what thin ice he's on. He'd do anything to make sure he qualifies for early retirement."

"Not this," I say stoutly. "I admit Zachary hasn't been the greatest teacher up until now, but his integrity has never been in question. Even at his very lowest point, he never claimed to be anything that he wasn't. There's a difference in those kids now. It's not just Zachary. The phys ed coaches see it. The lunchroom monitors see it. Emma Fountain sees it. *I* see it. They're not angels, but they're *better*. They go on field trips. A local business leader has taken them under his wing."

"What local business leader?"

"Jake Terranova," I admit. "I know it's a little odd—"

He laughs mirthlessly. "Spare me. I reject this so-called wonder of yours. In fact"—he takes out a large ring binder and begins flipping pages—"I've been reviewing the district contract. I'm sure you're familiar with Article Twelve, Subsection Nine."

"Refresh my memory," I reply warily.

He smiles. "It states that any teacher presiding over declining test grades in a core subject for three straight years can be deemed an ineffective educator and fired for cause."

I'm appalled. "You mean Zachary? He's been moved around so much that you couldn't possibly blame any class's failing grades on him."

"There's a formula," he explains. "You calculate a baseline using past performances of the individual kids. And it just so happens that Mr. Kermit's students have shown declining results on the state science exam for the past two years. If the assessment at the end of this month goes the same way, then I've got him."

I don't even watch my words. "That's so unfair!"

He raises one jet-black eyebrow. "How can you of all people say that? You just told me that he's turned this class around. If that's true, they'll ace the test, and Mr. Kermit will have nothing to worry about."

I bite my tongue. This man is my boss. He speaks for the school district, and what he says goes. He may be a stinker, but that doesn't change the fact that it's everybody's job to carry out his instructions.

Besides, he's just being sarcastic, but in this case he happens to be right. Zachary really *has* transformed that class. They don't have to "ace" the science test; they just have to beat their scores from past years. How hard can that be? Tests like this one got them placed in SCS-8 in the first place.

I leave the office feeling a lot better about Zachary's chances of making it through till June. Still, it can't hurt to pass on a suggestion that he might want to do some extra test prep for the coming science assessment. Forewarned is forearmed.

Zachary Kermit is too good a teacher to lose his retirement just because a certain cranky superintendent can't forgive him for something that was never his fault in the first place.

# Twenty-Three
## Kiana Roubini

"**C**ut it out, Chauncey!"

My half-pint half brother is crawling all over my notes, which are spread out around me on the floor of the den. His onesy is open, his diaper is sagging, and he's teething and drooling, an action figure of a Power Ranger or Transformer clutched in his little fist. Mateo can probably ID it—I make a mental note to Snapchat him a picture.

Chauncey's chubby knee comes down on my chart

of the atomic masses of elements, shredding the paper, and I freak out.

*"Louise!"* I bellow. Then, borrowing Dad's line: *"Jeez, Louise!"*

Chauncey is startled and bursts into tears. I feel bad about that. Pesky as he is, you can't help getting used to a cute little guy who seems to love you for no logical reason. On the other hand, I *need* my chart of atomic masses just like I need my periodic table, and all the other notes I have carefully organized on the floor.

I'll never understand teachers. Sure, I get it that Mr. Kermit has come back from the Lost Land of Crossword Puzzles. But now, totally out of nowhere, he's gone science crazy.

"The state science assessment is on October twenty-third," he announced last week. "This is our chance to prove that our class can do as well as any other group. Maybe even better than some."

The way he said it—how he made it sound like it was us against everybody else who calls us unteachable— got the whole class on board the Science Express.

Elaine's eyes were practically shining with excitement and purpose. Maybe she thought we were going to dissect somebody.

"We're like Frodo going up against the dark forces

of Middle Earth," Mateo declared.

Okay, that's standard Mateo. But even Aldo is sort of into it. Ribbit is framing this as a giant *in-your-face* to the whole school. No way Aldo can pass up a chance at that.

So that's why I'm in the den, up to my ears in graphs and formulas, yelling at a baby. You think I'm thrilled about it? The best thing about being a short-timer is you can slack off with no consequences. And I can't even get that right.

"What's wrong?" Stepmonster rushes in and spies her little darling laying waste to my work like Godzilla stomping Tokyo—oh man, I really am spending too much time with Mateo!

She expertly scoops him up using one arm.

I almost bark something rude like "What took you so long?" But then I spot the tall glass of iced tea in her other hand.

"I thought you could use a study break," she offers, setting the drink down on the edge of the coffee table. "Kiana, your dad and I are so proud of how hard you've been working lately."

It annoys me. Who does she think she is—my mother?

She's definitely not that. I know because she isn't on

a movie set in Utah, leaving me in exile.

Chauncey hangs off her hip, arms and legs flailing. The action figure flies from his little hand, landing with a *ker-plop* in my iced tea.

"Chauncey!" she scolds. "You ruined your sister's drink!"

Believe it or not, I actually sympathize with her then—overworked, sleep-deprived, and saddled with her husband's California kid.

"It's not ruined," I say quickly. "It's just—" I fish the Power Ranger out, watching the level of tea go down. I drop it back in again, and the level rises. My eyes widen in understanding. "Archimedes' first law of buoyancy—a floating object displaces its own weight in liquid! I've been trying to understand it all day!" I spring up and wrap my arms around Stepmonster. "Thanks for the tea!"

Chauncey sinks his newly cut tooth into his thumb and starts bawling again.

The science craze even extends to Terranova Motors. Jake buys these rolling whiteboards, and his mechanics show us how to calculate horsepower and torque. We have a contest to see who can be the quickest to label the parts of an internal combustion engine. Parker wins, even though some of his spellings are a little creative, like CRANKSHAFT = SCARFTHANK.

Jake keeps telling us how important it is to do well on the test to make Mr. Kermit look good. He says it over and over again, until his face gets flushed like he's really stressed about it. What's the big deal? If, by some miracle, we ace the exam, those good grades will be ours, not our teacher's. And if we bomb out— well, that'll be on us too. How is it Mr. Kermit's fault if his class happens to be dumb at science?

Or maybe we're not so dumb. On Friday, we take a practice test, and we do pretty well. I pull off a 92, which is amazing, considering science isn't my best subject. Elaine gets an 86, and both Barnstorm and Rahim crack 70. Even Mateo squeaks out a pass at 67, which isn't bad for someone who can't tell the difference between Earth and Middle Earth, and thinks the Force and magic are real.

Aldo brings up the rear with a 62, but Mr. Kermit steps in before he can get too worked up about it.

"Think about it, Aldo—three more points and you would have *passed*. You're a completely different student now. You're reading *Where the Red Fern Grows*, an award-winning novel. I believe in you. And on test day, I know you'll be able to scrounge up three more points."

"Yeah!" Aldo exclaims, energized. "If I can care whether Old Dan and Little Ann win the coon hunt, I can care about anything! Even stupid science!"

"Puffy-tails for everybody!" crows Barnstorm, waving a crutch in the air.

"Let's not get ahead of ourselves," our teacher tells us. "We don't want to be overconfident for the real test next week. But," he adds, "I'm proud of each and every one of you. If you put up these kinds of scores on the actual assessment, it'll say a lot about what we've accomplished together as a class."

Those words stick with me: *what we've accomplished together as a class.*

Well, okay, I'm part of the *accomplishment*—but I'm not actually part of the *class.* Technically, I'm not even part of the *school.*

It doesn't make any real difference. I'm going home to LA, but not next week. I'll be taking the science assessment alongside everybody else.

Still, I can't help wondering how the others would react if they knew the truth about me. It makes me uneasy. I can't get past the guilty feeling that I'm keeping a secret from my friends.

## Twenty-Four
### Barnstorm Anderson

Just when you think you've got it figured out, everything changes.

First, life's about scoring touchdowns, shooting baskets, hitting home runs—until you get injured for the rest of middle school, which might as well be five hundred years.

Then life's about having a sweet row of thirty-seven puffy-tails, three times as many as anybody else. But pretty soon, nobody cares about that either.

Now it's all science, all the time. My head is stuffed so full of facts that I can't blow my nose for fear it'll come out paradichlorobenzene. I've stopped watching TV, because any new information going in might push out something that's already there. My parents think I'm nuts; *I* think I'm nuts. I'm definitely not me anymore. But when that test happens, I'm going to be ready.

And then life changes again. On test day, I thump out of the house, swinging on my crutches, just in time to see the school bus disappearing around the corner.

*"Hey—!"* I'm so shocked that, for a second, I forget about my injury and try to sprint after it, landing face-first on the sidewalk. By the time I pick myself up again, the bus is out of sight.

"No!" My eyes turn back to home. Mom had to work early this morning, so there's no one to bum a ride from. I'm in agony—and not just because my nose is bleeding. You know the phrase "It's no skin off my nose"? Well, there's actual skin off my actual nose!

But the worst part is I've studied for this test more than I've studied for every other test combined, going back to kindergarten. And I'm going to miss it! The others will kill me—and that includes Elaine, who might really do it!

Out of options, I start hobbling along the sidewalk in the direction of school. There's no chance I'll make it, but what choice do I have?

I'm thumping and swinging at maximum speed when one car engine roars above the others. From our many field trips to Terranova Motors, I recognize the sound of a broken muffler. An old pickup truck is zooming along in the right lane, passing cars on the inside. To my surprise, I recognize it from vuvuzela-dumping day. It's Parker's pickup! I spot him behind the wheel, beside some old lady in the passenger seat.

Saved!

Without thinking, I step into the road, waving both crutches over my head. With a screech of brakes and burning rubber, he comes to a halt about three inches from my skinless nose.

Parker rolls down the window. "Get out of the way, Barnstorm! I'm in a hurry!"

I yank open the passenger door. "Me too! I missed the bus! You've got to give me a ride to school!"

"I can't!" he protests. "I'm not allowed. I can only drive for farm business!"

"What about her?" I demand, indicating the old lady.

"That's different! That's my grams. I have to take her to the hospital!"

Grams—who seems fine to me—shoves over and pats the seat beside her. "Hop in, kiddo!"

For some reason, that drives Parker crazy. "He's not kiddo! *I'm* kiddo!"

I climb up to the seat, pulling the crutches in after me, and shut the door. Aggravated, Parker stomps on the gas and we lurch away, sideswiping a garbage can at the curb. I guess you don't have to be a very good driver to get a provisional license, compared to a real one.

As we approach the hospital, Parker cranes his neck. "We need the entrance that says EMERGENCY—I'll probably read it wrong, but you'll see it regular."

"You might see it regular too now," I remind him. Parker has been seeing a special reading teacher, and he's supposedly making a ton of progress.

"There—emergency!" We wheel onto a driveway.

"You got it!" I congratulate him. "But what's the emergency? Your grandma looks fine."

Grams peers at me. "Your nose is bleeding. You should see a doctor about that."

"She's not fine," Parker insists. "She's walking funny. Duck!" he adds as we approach a police officer on my side.

So I bow down out of sight, and that's when I spot the old lady's white Nikes.

"You'd walk funny too," I tell Parker. "She's got her shoes on the wrong feet."

We pull over and Grams switches sneakers. Lo and behold, she walks fine.

So we drop her at the senior center, and Parker and I head to school.

"You're welcome," I tell him. "You could have been sitting in emergency all day and missed the science test."

"I shouldn't be driving you," he retorts resentfully. "If I get pulled over, I could lose my provisional license."

But we don't get pulled over. We've even got a few minutes to spare before school starts. I thank him for the ride, and he thanks me for looking at his grandmother's feet. He's not a bad kid. We've gotten to know each other pretty well since being in SCS-8.

We're on our way to room 117, when the door of the boys' room opens and out steps Mateo.

"Hey," we both greet him.

He doesn't answer, which is weird. Mateo usually talks at the speed of light—186,000 miles per second, in case it comes up on the science test. His expression is weird too—embarrassed? Upset? I look down. The kid is standing in a puddle. Water drips from his clothes and even the tips of his fingers.

I'm mystified. "Dude, why are you all wet?"

My answer comes when three big guys emerge from the bathroom, shoving each other and laughing. I know them. They're football players—my teammates, not that they want anything to do with me now that I'm on the sidelines. It doesn't take a genius to figure out they're the reason Mateo's half-drowned.

The biggest of them, Faulkner, nods in my direction. "Anderson," he mumbles, and starts away.

I stick out a crutch and stop him. "Get the others," I tell Parker. He runs off in the direction of room 117, and I turn back to my former teammates. "Real nice. Picking on a kid a tenth your size, three on one."

"Like you never did it," sneers another of the three, Karnosky.

"I did it. Once." Last year. It was stupid. I just wanted to prove my aim was better than Karnosky's. The trick is to stick your finger in the faucet and direct the stream of water with deadly accuracy at the target.

But when I saw the kid I hit, dripping and miserable, I never did it again.

Besides, I didn't know that kid. I know Mateo.

"So you've got nothing to say," Faulkner grunts. "What's this dweeb to you, anyway?"

"His name is Mateo," I say stubbornly.

I hear footsteps in the hall behind me—Parker leading the rest of SCS-8. I don't actually see them, but I know they're there. My attention stays focused on the three football players.

Faulkner looks surprised. "Wait—you're with *them*? The Unteachables?"

"They're better friends than I ever had when I hung out with you!" I spit back.

Karnosky kicks the crutch out from under my left arm, knocking me off-balance. Rahim catches me just in time to keep me from hitting the wet floor. Aldo leaps forward and shoves Karnosky back against the wall. It's a dumb move—typical Aldo. Karnosky is as mean as they come, and Aldo isn't nearly as tough against real people as he is against lockers, which don't hit back.

Sure enough, the third kid, Bellingham, takes a swing at Aldo, and I'm thinking: *Here we go* . . .

But Aldo ducks, and a big body steps into the path

of the flying fist. The heavy blow lands on Elaine's shoulder. It makes a loud smack, but she doesn't budge, solid as an oak tree.

Bellingham's eyes widen in horror as he realizes who he's hit. Faulkner and Karnosky turn pale.

I get the feeling Faulkner's tempted to snarl something like "This isn't over." But Elaine rhymes with pain. He wants it to be over.

The three football players turn tail and flee.

I bray a laugh at their receding backs. "Gee, guys, can't you run away any faster?"

Kiana starts hustling the lot of us toward room 117. "Lucky for us there weren't any teachers around."

"Lucky for *us*?" I crow. "Lucky for those jerks! Elaine was about to stomp them into hamburger."

"Me?" Elaine asks, confused.

"We should have let you wipe up the floor with them," I enthuse. "You know, like that kid you knocked unconscious and duct-taped to the flagpole."

Elaine looks totally bewildered.

"Or when you tipped the steam table over onto the lunch ladies because you didn't like crunchy peanut butter," Rahim adds.

"I love crunchy peanut butter," Elaine rumbles.

"What about the guy you head-butted down the stairs?" I demand. "You can't say that never happened! Like twenty people wound up in the nurse's office!"

"He just dropped his phone," she explains. "He bent to pick it up. I bent to help him. We bumped heads." Elaine assumes a faraway expression as she relives the moment. "The kids on the steps didn't stand a chance. He took them all out on his way down. It looked like a giant wave of people breaking over the staircase."

We end up standing there outside room 117, staring at each other in amazement.

"It's just rumors, you guys," Kiana tells us. "You know how stories spread in a school."

"The uprooted tree?" Parker persists. "The bathroom stall door? The fire extinguisher? Come on, the fire extinguisher has to be true."

Elaine shakes her head. "Sorry."

"Okay, fine," I say finally. "But it has to stay our secret. If word gets out that you aren't a doomsday machine, the entire football team's going to kick our butts."

Ribbit appears in the doorway. "What's everybody doing out here? The science test starts in three minutes."

The science test! After all the craziness of the morning, I almost forgot about it. Who knows how many important facts already leaked out of my head?

Ribbit distributes the test booklets as we take our seats.

It's game on.

# Twenty-Five
## Kiana Roubini

The first time the Unteachables go to Sonic is the day of the state science assessment. We don't know if we'll be able to celebrate how we did, but we can definitely celebrate the fact that it's over and we survived. Plus, Parker has his family's pickup, so we can use the drive-thru.

Of course, he's not allowed to have passengers except his grandmother, so we have to walk and meet him there. But we can drink our slushes and sodas in the flatbed, lounging among the bushel baskets of potatoes and onions. It's pretty fun, so we go back a couple of days later when the weather's still nice.

It's a long walk home, though. So it's pretty late in the afternoon when I come stumbling through the door, hyped up on sugar, to find Stepmonster in the front hall waiting for me.

I'm instantly on my guard. I've been in Greenwich more than a month, and she's never once waited for me. She's always too busy chasing after Chauncey, trying to keep him from spontaneously combusting, or flushing himself down the toilet, or whatever.

"What?" I ask her.

"Your school called," she tells me grimly. "Or maybe I should say *a* school called, since you don't really go there."

My first instinct is to try to bluff through it. "Of course it's my school. Where do you think I hang out every day?"

"Save it, Kiana. It's all out in the open now. That science exam you've been working so hard on—they graded your test, but couldn't find a student to match it to. They called us because we're the only Roubinis in Greenwich. You're busted."

The science test! I should have known. Just because

Mr. Kermit never checks his class list doesn't mean nobody else checks theirs.

I kick off my sneakers and stomp into the living room. Wouldn't you know it—Chauncey is fast asleep in his playpen. The one time I need him awake and alert and ripping the curtains down, he fails me.

"It's not my fault," I complain. "You left me alone on the first day of school, so I found a class and stayed there."

Believe it or not, Stepmonster actually looks a little bit ashamed. "I'm sorry. I should have been a little more on top of things. But your education isn't a game, and a school is more than a drop-in center where you can come and go as you please. Why in a million years would you think you could get away with this?"

"Because nobody cares about me!" I explode. "If you did, you wouldn't have flaked off before making sure I got registered. And anyway, what difference does it make? My real school is in LA. Nobody's going to sweat what happened during the few weeks I was here. This isn't my home; it's just a place to park me until Mom gets done in Utah!"

For a split second, Stepmonster looks as if she's about to cry. But she doesn't. I'll always appreciate her for that, because I definitely would have cried too.

"Dad and I know you live with your mom," she says at last. "But this is your home too—and we're your family."

I peer over at her. She really thinks that? News to me. I mean, she's always *nice*, when she isn't too distracted by her kid—who, admittedly, is a full-time job. But *family*?

"So what happens now?" I ask in a small voice.

"I do what I should have done on day one," she decides. "I'm going to the school to get you properly registered."

"No!" I howl. "They'll put me in regular classes! They won't let me stay in SCS-8!"

"Why not?"

"Because—because"—I blurt out the only thing I can think of—"because I'm not dumb enough!"

She's blown away. "*Dumb* enough?"

I spill my guts—the Unteachables and Mr. Kermit, and how we started out a bad class, but we're turning into an amazing one, and pretty good friends besides.

Stepmonster listens to my sob story, and the longer I go on, the more stunned she seems. By the time I get to the end of it, Chauncey is awake. But instead of fussing, he's watching me through the mesh of the playpen, listening intently, like he can't wait to hear how it all turns out.

Stepmonster looks me straight in the eye. "If that's the class you want, that's the class you're going to be in, unteachable or not."

I jump up and wrap my arms around her. I don't know if she expected it, but I definitely didn't. It's a weird moment, but not totally in a bad way.

Chauncey isn't a big fan of that. He screams his head off.

I pull back. "You'd better go get him. In his mind, hugging privileges are his and his alone."

She laughs. "You're probably right. And by the way, I don't think you're very unteachable. That science test? The school says you aced it."

# Twenty-Six

## Mr. Kermit

I never thought it could be like this again.

Every morning, as I park the Coco Nerd—good as new; or at least good as twenty-seven years old—I can't wait to get into the classroom. There's a spring in my step; I'm practically jogging. At the coffeepot in the faculty lounge, I fill the Toilet Bowl only halfway. I don't need coffee to stay awake. I'm firing on all cylinders, as Jumping Jake Terranova might say. Even that name doesn't sour me the way it once did.

I'll never be able to forgive the cheating scandal, but there's no denying the role Jake played in turning the class around.

The class! Just the thought of them sends a jolt of electricity up my spine. Who could have guessed that the rejects of the whole district would turn out to be exactly what I needed? The Unteachables! Well, not anymore. Oh, sure, there are better students in this world—okay, there are better students in this hallway. But comparing what they've become to what they started out as, it's clear that something very special is happening. And their teacher has to believe in something I haven't believed in for a long time: myself.

It was the state science assessment that did it for me. There was a moment at the beginning—Parker in his usual pose, hunched low over his exam booklet, staring as if trying to see inside the individual molecules of paper.

"Hose hypnotists . . . ," he was mumbling, struggling to make sense of the letters on the page. "Hose hypnotists . . ." Then all those hours of reading support kicked in. "Photosynthesis!" he exclaimed triumphantly.

I had to hold myself back from cheering out loud.

Jake actually took test day off so he could be with

the class to provide "moral support." In reality, he was more stressed out than the students and putting everybody on edge. Eventually, I had to coax him into the hall and tell him to go back to his dealership.

He protested. "But what if . . . they . . . you . . ." Bereft of speech, he threw his arms around me. This was not something I ever wanted to happen.

"Go," I told him, wriggling free. "Sell cars. Jump through hoops."

"You're the best teacher ever," Jake declared emotionally. "I'm so sorry I did, you know, the *thing*."

"Goodbye, Jake."

More memories of that morning: looking out over my students and suddenly the whole room was blurry because my eyes were filled with tears. Just like they dove into the river because they thought I was drowning, they dove into this, and they did it for me. They had no way of knowing my job was on the line. That made it all the more impressive. I said this was important, and the kids took my word for it. They even *studied*! As I walked between the desks, peering over shoulders, the scratch of number 2 pencils filling in ovals made my heart swell to bursting.

I knew it then, and the feeling has only gotten stronger since: I *love* these students. Parker, Aldo, Elaine,

Barnstorm, Rahim, and Mateo. And Kiana, who, it turns out, isn't even really in the class—or any class.

That's my fault. I'm the one who never bothered to glance at my own attendance list long enough to realize that my top student wasn't on it. How blind I was! How burned-out and detached! On the other hand, who expects a kid to come to a school she isn't signed up for?

"Her stepmother straightened everything out," Christina Vargas explains at our meeting the week after the test. "Kiana's only here for a couple of months, and the registration process was too much red tape. So she blundered into your class and figured she'd be gone by the time anybody figured out she didn't belong. It's ridiculous, but almost understandable."

My cheeks get hot. "I suppose that doesn't make me look very on top of things."

"We're all at fault," the principal says kindly. "I had her progress report right in my hand. I remember struggling to put a face to the name, but I never took it any further."

"Well, I'm not sorry it happened," I go on. "She's a fantastic kid and a brilliant student. Look at her score on the exam—ninety-six. She sets a positive example for the rest of the class . . ." My voice trails off.

Christina's face has turned ashen. I take a guess at the reason. "Are you moving her? Because her science score proves she doesn't belong with my kids?"

"I'm not moving her," she replies grimly. "Her step-mother specifically asked that Kiana stay with you. Demanded, actually. But there's something else."

I sit back, waiting.

Christina takes a deep breath. "This is difficult, Zachary. I hate to be the person who has to give you the news. The truth is, you won't be a teacher here much longer."

It comes so far out of left field that I'm shocked into silence at first. Then light dawns: "Thaddeus? The science test? But the scores were *good*! Kiana's alone—"

"That's just it," she tells me. "You know Dr. Thaddeus wants you gone. As soon as he realized what was happening with the Roubini girl, he had her result disallowed."

"Even without her," I insist. "The others have made so much progress! Surely their grades are enough."

"Almost," she says sadly. "Remember, Dr. Thaddeus has access to every test these kids have taken since preschool. He can cherry-pick exactly the numbers he needs to make sure you can't win."

It reminds me of an old saying I heard somewhere: *Figures don't lie. But liars figure.*

Devastated, the principal removes an envelope from her desk drawer and hands it over. "Dr. Thaddeus dropped it off this morning. I pleaded with him, Zachary. I pointed out how close they came to making it, even though he stacked the odds against them. I raved about how absolute zero was expected of these kids, so any proficiency at all is a credit to a remarkable teacher. He couldn't have cared less. He said even if they had fallen short by one-millionth of one percent, it wouldn't have changed anything . . ."

She's still talking—weeping, practically—but I can't make out any of it. It's like I'm in a tunnel and the echoes are rattling around but not quite reaching me. Fingers numb, I fumble the letter out of the envelope.

## NOTICE OF TERMINATION
### ATT: Kermit, Zachary

Please be advised that, pursuant to Article 12, Subsection 9 of the Greenwich Teachers Association contract, your services will no longer be required as of December 22 of the current school year. . . .

My eyes skip down the page, bouncing off terms like "poor performance," "unacceptable results," and "ineffective educator." I can't bring myself to read it all, but the message is painfully clear. This magical semester—in which I turned my own life around as much as the students'—was nothing but a tease. It raised my hopes, only to dash them to pieces at my feet. It restored my faith in teaching and in myself purely so the taste would be all the more bitter now. I'm fired—sacked, kicked to the curb, canned, given the boot—as of December 22.

Merry Christmas.

Worst of all, my career is going to end six months too soon to qualify me for early retirement. Fade to black.

I barely hear Christina's tearful words of sympathy as I wander out of her office. Instead of heading to room 117, I stagger through the main doors and find the parking lot. I can't face the kids—not now, when I'm still so stunned. What would I say to them? How could I explain it? I don't blame them for the superintendent's malice, but how could I ever convince them that this isn't their fault? I'll have to find those words eventually, but not today.

The outside world sounds different than it usually

does—subdued, muffled. Somehow, my feet carry me to the Coco Nerd, and I climb behind the wheel—the locks haven't worked in more than a decade. The car starts in its customary cloud of burned oil. Outside, it begins to rain, and I activate the lone functioning wiper. Too bad it isn't the one on the driver's side. I squint through the water-spattered windshield. At least it's forcing me to watch the road. Otherwise, I'd probably wrap the Coco Nerd around a telephone pole.

At the entrance to the parking lot, I signal left and press the gas. There's a loud pop, followed by a clatter, and everything goes quiet. I try the key a few more times. Nothing. Not even a feeble attempt to catch. The turn signal clicks once more, and then it dies too.

I get out of the car and open the hood. To my amazement, nothing's there. On closer inspection, I spy the motor lying on the pavement next to the battery, the radiator, the transmission, and a lot of other stuff that used to be attached to the car. Over a quarter century with the Coco Nerd, and I thought I'd seen it all. Wrong again.

This is an ex–Coco Nerd.

It's raining harder and I'm getting soaked. There's probably something I should be doing, but what? Call a tow truck? Why? This heap of scrap metal isn't really a car anymore. Inform the school that their driveway is blocked? They'll figure it out sooner or later.

I flip up the collar of my jacket and start walking toward home.

# Twenty-Seven
## Kiana Roubini

The first day I'm officially a student in Mr. Kermit's class, Mr. Kermit doesn't even show up.

It doesn't bother us at first. It reminds me of the beginning of the year, when Ribbit was late every day. It takes a long time to fill a coffee cup the size of a bathtub.

I guess we get a little loud, but when Miss Fountain sticks her head into the room, we quiet down in a hurry.

She's frowning. "Where's Mr. Kermit?"

We stare back at her blankly. How should we know? We listen to her high heels clicking urgently down the hall.

"Do you think we're getting a sub?" asks Rahim.

"Please don't let it be Dawn of the Dead," Barnstorm groans.

Ten minutes later, we hear running footsteps in the corridor, and Jake Terranova bursts into room 117. "Hi, guys—sorry I'm late. Mr. Kermit can't make it today."

"Are you our sub?" Parker asks.

"Not exactly," he tells us. "But since you're coming to the dealership later anyway, Emma—Miss Fountain, I mean—well, why bring in a substitute for just a couple of hours?"

"Is that legal?" Mateo inquires.

"Technically, Miss Fountain is covering both classes. Think of me as an assistant. You know, a volunteer."

"Is Mr. Kermit sick?" Rahim asks.

"Nah!" Jake shrugs this off. "I mean, not *really*. He might be *upset* a little—"

I jump on that. "Upset about what?"

Jake is flustered. There's obviously something going on that we're not supposed to know about, and Jake has the kind of face that can't hide secrets. When you're the boss of a giant car dealership, you don't have to answer questions from your employees, because what you say goes. But that doesn't work with a bunch of kids.

"It's the science test, isn't it?" Aldo says belligerently. "I flunked and now Ribbit won't come to school."

Barnstorm cackles. "If that's how it went, you'd have been in an empty classroom your whole life."

"Is that it?" Elaine rumbles. "Did we fail the test?"

The babble of agitated voices grows louder until Jake waves his arms for quiet. He perches on the edge of the teacher's desk and motions us close. "Okay, I'll tell you. But you have to promise not to say anything to *her*." He motions over his shoulder in the direction of Miss Fountain's room.

What he reveals turns our blood to ice. Dr. Thaddeus—superintendent of the whole school district—has been out to get Mr. Kermit all year. He found a way to use our scores on the state science assessment to get Ribbit declared an incompetent teacher. He'll be out of a job at the end of this term.

"I knew it!" Aldo rages. "We flunked the test!"

"You *didn't*," Jake insists. "None of you did. It's a numbers game—if you fiddle with them enough, you

225

can get them to say almost anything."

"It's no game," I say bitterly. "It's our teacher, and he's getting fired for no reason."

"Who does that guy Thaddeus think he is?" Barnstorm growls.

"He's like Voldemort and Darth Vader rolled into one," Mateo adds.

Miss Fountain appears in the doorway. "Since Mr. Kermit's absent, I thought it would be nice if both classes shared Circle Time today."

She picked the worst possible time for that invitation. Circle Time? When our teacher's getting shafted? A chorus of protest begins in our throats—one that Jake silences by raising one warning finger.

"Circle Time sounds great, Em—uh, Miss Fountain," Jake accepts on our behalf. "We'll be right there."

It's the last thing we're in the mood for. How can the superintendent be so mean? Why would he even want to? Maybe Mr. Kermit was a lousy teacher back in the crossword puzzle era, but now he's the greatest!

As we grumble and seethe our way next door to room 115, I sidle up to Jake. "How can this be?" I ask in distress. "I know I got a ninety-six. And if everybody else passed, that shouldn't add up to failure no matter how much you crunch the numbers."

He looks at me sympathetically. "You have to understand, Kiana. You weren't a registered student on test day, so the ninety-six doesn't count."

I stumble into Miss Fountain's classroom, my mind a pinwheel. The news of the past few minutes has been a bomb blast, but this might be even worse. Our teacher is being fired, and sure, it's the superintendent's fault. It's the school's fault for not supporting Mr. Kermit. It might even be a little bit Jake's fault for that cheating scandal so long ago.

But mostly, it's *my* fault. If I was properly registered, Dr. Thaddeus would have to count my score. But no—I was a short-timer. This hick town and hick school had nothing to teach me. I was just passing through. What difference did it make what happened here?

Well, it's making a pretty big difference now!

By the time we take our seats on the floor around the circle, I feel like my head is about to explode. A nervous murmur comes from Miss Fountain's students. They can sense the emotional upset coming from the seven of us. Vladimir is beeping like a robot in one of Mateo's sci-fi movies, but Aldo is too wound up to respond to his reptilian friend.

227

Miss Fountain addresses the group: "Who would like to be first to contribute to our circle?"

It comes pouring out of me. "It isn't Mr. Kermit's fault that I never registered, and now he's getting fired, and it isn't fair—"

I've got more to say—a lot more. But my words trigger Aldo, who bursts out, "I hated all teachers until Ribbit came along! And teachers hated me! But then—"

"Everyone thought I was weird before Mr. Kermit's class!" Mateo blurts over him. "Like I was an android in a human world—"

"Ribbit's the only person who notices what I'm *good* at instead of just what I'm *bad* at—" Rahim adds to the clamor.

"I used to be stupid before Mr. Kermit!" barks Parker. "Nobody ever tried to get me any help—"

"This school only cared about me when I was scoring touchdowns!" Barnstorm blusters. "But Ribbit's *better* than that—"

Even strong, silent Elaine speaks up in her deep voice. "I never had any friends until this year—"

We're all talking at the same time, hollering to make ourselves heard. The seventh graders are really nervous. Vladimir is running crazed loops in his cage because Aldo's so upset. He's yelling louder than any of us, his red hair practically defying gravity.

Miss Fountain is trying to restore order, but no one is paying any attention to her. Finally, she inserts both index fingers into her mouth and unleashes an ear-splitting whistle that threatens to have plaster raining down on us from the ceiling. It isn't very Circle Time, but it gets the job done. Silence falls and we stare at the young teacher in awe. How did such a large noise come from such a small person?

"Thank you," she says, her quiet self again. "Now, where did you kids hear that Mr. Kermit won't be back after the end of this term?"

Nobody answers, but we all look over in Jake's direction. Miss Fountain glares at him.

He shrugs helplessly. "It just slipped out."

Miss Fountain takes a deep breath. "Mr. Terranova, please stay with my group while I take Mr. Kermit's students back to their own room. We've had enough Circle Time for today."

She sweeps us back to room 117.

"This is so unfair!" I'm still shaking with anger. "How can they do this to Mr. Kermit? How can they do it to *us*?"

Miss Fountain tries to be sympathetic and reasonable

at the same time. "I agree with you, Kiana. It's very upsetting. But there's nothing we can do about it. Even Principal Vargas—this is above her level too. It comes straight from the district office."

Parker is bitter. "Mr. Kermit helped every single one of us. And what can we do to help him back? A big fat zero!"

Something stirs in the back of my head—something I heard a long time ago. Something *Miss Fountain* said!

And then I have it. "The science fair!"

"What about it?" Barnstorm groans. "Haven't we had enough science for one lifetime?"

I turn to Miss Fountain. "Remember on the bus ride to Terranova Motors? When you tried to convince Mr. Kermit to have us enter the science fair?"

She looks annoyed. "That was *supposed* to be a private conversation."

"Well, I heard it. You told him the winning team gets ten points added to all their scores on the science assessment. Would that be enough to put us over the top and save Mr. Kermit's job?"

Suddenly, all eyes are on Miss Fountain, waiting for her answer.

"I'm sure it would," she says finally. "But remember— Mr. Kermit's answer was no to the science fair."

"Yeah, but that was before he got canned," Barnstorm reasons. "That changes everything, right?"

She shakes her head. "Mr. Kermit is a very private person. He wouldn't want you to take his personal problems onto yourselves."

"What if we don't tell him about it?" Rahim muses.

"Be serious," Miss Fountain insists. "He's still your teacher until the end of the term. How can you expect to do a science fair project and keep it a secret from him?"

"Terranova Motors!" I exclaim. "I bet Jake will let us work on it there. Miss Fountain, we can *do* this. I know we can."

By now, the others are grouped around me, and we're confronting Miss Fountain as if daring her to say no.

"Entering doesn't mean you're going to win," she reminds us.

"But not entering means we lose for sure," Mateo counters.

"It'll be a long shot," the teacher warns. "You don't even have a topic yet, and the other groups have already been working for weeks."

"So it's a yes?" I prompt.

The cheer that erupts when Miss Fountain nods

is loud enough to bring Jake running from the next room. He loves the idea and pledges to do everything he can to help us, courtesy of his dealership.

Rule 1, which Mateo calls the Prime Directive: Mr. Kermit is not allowed to know about our project. If he finds out, the deal is off.

We'll up our Terranova Motors visits to three afternoons per week. Miss Fountain will come with us if Mr. Kermit will look after her class. We'll work weekends too. Whatever it takes.

After lunch, Jake acts as our chaperone on the minibus over to the dealership. As excited as we are, the ride is somber. With Mr. Kermit's job on the line, the stakes are sky-high. And we haven't even started planning yet.

"Do you really think we can pull this off?" Parker asks dubiously. "Have you seen the kind of kids who enter the science fair? They're, like, *smart*."

"There are different kind of smarts," Jake puts in positively. "School is important, but there are things you can't learn from books."

"You mean the internet?" Mateo asks.

"I mean *street* smarts," Jake explains. "I was never the greatest student, but I knew how to scratch and claw and build a business. Trust me, you guys have street smarts coming out your ears. *That's* what's going to give you the perfect project."

"What's the project going to be?" Aldo asks.

"That's what we have to figure out," I say. "It can't be too simple, because we have to blow the judges away. But we don't have much time, either. The science fair is in three weeks."

The bus pulls up to the dealership's service area and we file out onto the pavement. We're about to enter the building when Parker points. "Hey, isn't that Mr. Kermit's car?"

We all look. On a flatbed tow truck parked outside the service bay sits the rusted remains of an ancient Chrysler that might have once been blue. Parts are strewn all around it, also rusted, some broken.

Jake sighs. "Poor guy. Like he doesn't have enough hanging over his head, now he has to take taxis to school."

"When's it going to get fixed?" Mateo asks.

"You don't fix something like that," Elaine remarks. "You give it a decent burial."

Jake nods. "I only towed it here to get it out of the school's driveway."

"Seems a shame to waste a whole car," Parker muses.

"That's no car," Barnstorm retorts. "It's a pile of

garbage. It was garbage even when Ribbit was still driving it."

"Have some respect for the dead," I put in morosely.

"Respect," Jake echoes wanly. "Emma says her mom picked out that Chrysler. It's older than she is."

Mateo pipes up. "You know the part in *Harry Potter* where Mr. Weasley uses magic to enchant an old car to make it fly?"

"Not now, Mateo." I try to say it kindly. "We have to come up with a topic for our science fair project."

"Well, that's just it," he insists. "The car needs respect, and we need a project. All that's missing is a little magic."

# Twenty-Eight

## Mr. Kermit

The minutes blur into hours, which blur into days, which blur into weeks.

The first thing the condemned man loses is his sense of time. All I know is that it's flying by too fast.

For so long, I couldn't wait to be finished with my teaching career. Now—barreling full speed and out of control toward the finish line—all I want to do is make it last.

It's tough to tell the kids that I won't be back after

Christmas, but they take it better than I expected. Maybe they already know—the rumor mill in a middle school can be like that.

They're the ones who changed everything for me. The "Unteachables." Ha! That's what happens when you put a closed-minded bully like Thaddeus in charge—a school district where wonderful students are tossed aside like the trash.

Parker—the kid has a reading problem, nothing more. The fact that no teacher ever bothered to find that out says more against the Greenwich schools than any cheating scandal.

Barnstorm—look at what they let him get away with because he happened to be a sports star. He never learned how to work before because he never had to.

Elaine—I'm as guilty as anybody for taking so long to figure out that Elaine is smart. And she is. She's also good at hiding it. Her reputation doesn't help. But teachers are supposed to see around things like that.

Mateo—the school jumped to conclusions about the kid's quirky personality. They wrote him off. He deserves better.

Rahim was allowed to sleep and doodle through sixth and seventh grade before he was dumped into SCS-8. Today, he's an absolute star over at the community college, but what's more important is how well he's doing in eighth grade.

Aldo might be the only one who belongs in SCS-8. But he's come a long, long way. He passed that science test—and the fact that he did isn't half as amazing as the fact that he even bothered to try.

Finally Kiana. She never had any business being in the class. She just drifted in and stayed. And not a single faculty member—myself included—bothered to look into who she was and what she was doing there. True, it worked out in the end. Kiana is a huge part of what went right in room 117. But she could just as easily have fallen through the cracks, and all her potential would have been wasted.

What's going to happen to the kids on December 22 when I have to leave? Kiana will be fine. She'll be back in California, and anyway, a bright girl like that will find a way to succeed wherever she ends up. But what about the others? Will the class get a real teacher, or will the replacement be a babysitter? Or worse, a warden? It's too easy to see the progress of the past weeks being rolled back. Christina will try to do right by the students. But in the end, Dr. Thaddeus calls the shots. He might even kibosh the trips to Terranova Motors, which mean so much to the kids.

It hurts to admit it, but the transformation of SCS-8 never could have happened without Jake. Part of it's the field trips, the time away from school. For kids like Aldo and Parker, the things they learned about cars are among the first things they ever learned, period. Or at least, learned without hating it. It might have started out as Jake trying to make up for his misdeeds of twenty-seven years ago, but he's taken a real interest in those kids, and they know it. When someone cares about you, it's natural to respond.

Strange that the man who used to be twelve-year-old Jake should star in my teaching rebirth. And his costar? Even stranger—Emma Fountain, daughter of my fiancée who married someone else. Emma may be a fish out of water in middle school, with her bucket-filling and her Goodbunnies. But her energy and enthusiasm are boundless and pure. She awakened a love of teaching in me that was buried before she was even born.

Lately, I've been covering Emma's classes while she takes the SCS-8 group over to the dealership. I can't bring myself to go there anymore. I've made a kind of peace with Jake, even started to like him a little. But it doesn't change the fact that he's the reason Dr.

Thaddeus developed his grudge way back when. Better to stay here in room 115, running Circle Time and playing nursemaid to Vladimir.

Emma's students are okay. Mostly there are just too many of them. Forty-three minutes go by, a bell rings, and a new crew is sitting there, looking exactly like the old crew. I can't tell them apart—not like the Unteachables, who are so distinctive and full of personality. Nobody is likely to mistake Aldo or Elaine for any other middle schooler.

As the weeks fly past and December 22 looms closer, I savor my time with the kids the way a gourmet lingers over a fine soufflé. The class is spending so many afternoons at Terranova Motors these days that they're almost lost to me already. They leave on the minibus at eleven and barely make it back before the three-thirty bell.

I read and reread Kiana's essays, lingering over her well-reasoned arguments; I relish the discussions with Elaine and Aldo as they work their way through *Where the Red Fern Grows*; I listen for the faint sound of Parker whistling through his teeth, a surefire sign that he's reading without having to struggle over every word. I cherish these things because I know I won't have them much longer.

At this point, every puffy-tail I award may well be my last.

At home, the walls of the apartment are closing in on me.

It never bothered me before, but it's driving me crazy now. This is the future, kicking around these two and a half rooms, one bath. I was planning to cash it in at the end of this year anyway. But with early retirement, I would have been able to redecorate, maybe even move to a nicer place in a better part of town. For sure I would have traveled. I might not have the money for that now. And anyway, I'm so down that I can't think of a single spot on this green Earth that I'm interested in visiting.

Of course, I could look for a new job. There are other schools in America. But Thaddeus has pretty much taken care of that. How do you explain to a prospective employer that you were fired for cause? Any Google search of the name Zachary Kermit will eventually spit out the words *cheating scandal*, and that'll be a deal breaker. Besides, at fifty-five, I'm not exactly a spring chicken. Starting over from scratch isn't a very attractive option.

Saturday morning. I shuffle into the kitchen to investigate the prospects for breakfast. A cheese stick and a semi-stale dinner roll. I've stopped food shopping again. I was doing okay for a while, but the bad news jolted me into old ways. Oh well, with coffee, it should at least go down and stay there.

Breakfast is interrupted by a series of clicks. It's the doorbell—or what would be the doorbell if the doorbell worked. Must be a mistake. Nobody ever comes to visit, and I haven't ordered anything.

I pad barefoot to the door and peer through the peephole into the smiling face of Emma Fountain. What does she want at eight o'clock on a Saturday morning?

She says, "Don't pretend you're not home, Mr. Kermit. I can hear you walking around in there."

I open the door. "What brings you here so early?"

"I've come to give you a ride to the science fair," she replies, as if it's the most obvious thing in the world.

"I'm not going to the science fair," I tell her. "I'm not feeling very warm and fuzzy toward that school these days."

"But you can't miss it!" she pleads. "What about the kids?"

"What kids? *My* kids? They won't be there. Nobody entered."

She looks evasive. "That might not be exactly true."

The coffee is getting cold. "Of course it's true. I'm their teacher. Don't you think I would have noticed if one of them was working on a science project?"

"They did it as a group."

"I repeat: not possible."

She drops the bombshell. "They've been working on it at the dealership."

It strikes a chord. The frequent extended trips to Terranova Motors. Emma accompanying the kids so I won't see what's going on. They've been doing this behind my back. It all fits—except for one gigantic question—

"But *why*?"

"They did it for *you*," she announces.

"For *me*? Why in a million years would they think I'd want them to—"

Then I remember: that random district policy—ten points added to the science scores of all winners. That would be enough to—

"They're trying to save my job!"

She beams. "Isn't it wonderful?"

"No!" I explode. "It means the kids blame themselves

for what happened. How would they even know about the connection to their test results?"

She studies the threadbare carpet.

"You had no right to tell them that!" I rave. "It's a gross violation of my privacy. Worse, it made them feel pressured to enter a science fair they have no chance of winning!"

"Don't be mad at them—"

"I'm not mad at them," I exclaim. "I'm mad at *you*! They could never do this on their own. You set this up—you and that Terranova dimwit!"

"Jake loves you."

"Yeah? Well, I tremble to see what would happen if he hated me!"

She puts on an expression I remember from Fiona— the *I'm-not-taking-no-for-an-answer* face.

"Okay," Emma concedes, "so maybe we weren't totally up front with you. But your kids are at school ready to present their project. And if you're not there to support them, you're never going to forgive yourself."

She doesn't fight fair. "Pour yourself a cup of coffee," I say. "I'll get dressed."

Surrender. Total and unconditional. I might as well get used to it.

Jake is waiting outside in the Porsche. "Hi, Mr. Kermit. Long time no see."

I scowl at him. He's a partner in this deception, and deserves no better. Plus, with an entire car dealership at his disposal, he chose to bring this motorized roller skate.

*For the students*, I remind myself, squeezing into the tiny back seat.

All the way to school, Jake keeps up a steady stream of conversation, ignoring frantic signaling from Emma to keep his big mouth shut.

"How about those kids doing this project on their own?" he enthuses. "They're really something!"

I'm too angry to answer. It's also possible that I'm too contorted in the back seat to make any sound. I'm getting reacquainted with my knees, which are pressed up against my chest.

When the Porsche reaches Greenwich Middle School, it takes the two of them to drag me out of the car.

A banner over the front entrance declares:

GREENWICH PUBLIC SCHOOLS
SCIENCE FAIR
DISTRICT CHAMPIONSHIPS

The parking lot is packed. The school halls bustle with students and parents. I forgot how popular the science fair is. I knew once, back when I cared about such things.

Walking stiffly—zombie style—after the tight car ride, I lumber inside, following Emma and Jake into the gym, which is the epicenter. The large space is filled with long tables, and colorful displays stretch as far as the eye can see. Students stand like sentries in front of their projects, excited and nervous, ready to face the judges.

It's been a rotten day so far, but as soon as I spot the kids of SCS-8, I feel the corners of my mouth turning upward. Even though I'm against this science fair idea 100 percent, I couldn't be more proud. My Unteachables did this for me. Okay, I won't be their teacher for long, but I'm their teacher today, and I intend to act like it.

Seeing me, their faces light up, and I smile wider. I must be losing my mind. A real teacher would be chewing them out, not beaming at them. I beam anyway, because they look so thrilled with themselves—Kiana, Aldo, Barnstorm, Mateo, Rahim, and Elaine.

I approach the group. "Where's Parker?"

"With his grandmother," Kiana supplies. "You'll see him soon."

Ah, the famous Grams. Some things never change. "Well, let's have a look at this top secret project."

I turn my attention to the display board behind them. The title is *The Internal Combustion Engine*. Obviously, the idea came from working at Terranova Motors. There are several fantastic drawings and diagrams done by Rahim. They're so professional that I wonder if the judges will believe it's real student work.

Beyond that—my heart sinks a little—the project is pretty thin. There's an information booklet with a few pages that could have been copied from any automotive web page. That's it. No working motor in a study that's supposed to be all about them. Not even a model of one.

I picture some of the other displays on the labyrinth of tables throughout the double gym. There's a miniature wind turbine and batteries that store the electricity it generates, a Foucault pendulum, a replica of the internal gyroscope that provides telemetry guidance for a ballistic missile. Everywhere, microscopes peer down at single-celled organisms, Geiger counters click, test tubes bubble, and static electricity jumps up Jacob's ladders. These projects come from the most talented science students in the entire district, not just Greenwich Middle School. *The Internal Combustion Engine* is a nice effort, but it doesn't come close to anything else here. This is like entering a grape into competition against a two-hundred-pound watermelon at the state fair.

Anger surges inside me. Maybe Jake doesn't know any better, but surely Emma understands that *The Internal Combustion Engine* doesn't stand the chance of an ice cube in molten lava against the other projects here. I take in the proud, hopeful faces of the Unteachables. It goes without saying that they're about to finish dead last. They could very well be laughed out of the competition. The blow could destroy their confidence and undo most of the progress of the past weeks.

The judges are at the very next table, practically chortling with glee as they watch a small robot shoot baskets at a Nerf hoop built into the giant crate that is the display. Two men and a woman—the high school science teachers along with a professor from the local college. They make notes on their clipboards, but there's no mistaking the enjoyment on their faces.

Not for long, I think, as the threesome approaches *The Internal Combustion Engine.*

The kids are so amped that you can almost hear a

power hum emanating from them. I feel a little sick. I resolve then and there to make a big stink if the judges are unkind about the project. Why not? There's no downside. What can they do—complain to Thaddeus and get me fired?

To my relief, the three are respectful and professional. They're obviously not very impressed, but they go through the motions of examining the display. They even come up with a few questions to ask.

The college professor reads through the booklet and comes to the last page—I never made it that far. There are exactly two words, written in large block capitals:

## LOOK OUTSIDE
———————→

An arrow points toward the gym's corner exit, which opens out to the parking lot.

The man frowns. "What does this mean?"

Elaine's deep baritone supplies the answer. "Maybe it means, you know, look outside."

"This way!" adds Barnstorm, thump-swinging on his crutches toward the door. The judges follow, herded like cattle by the rest of the class.

"What's going on?" I whisper to Emma.

She smiles at me, misty-eyed. "That would spoil the surprise."

Jake is grinning, which is almost worse than her kindergarten ways. I am so not in the mood.

I step out of the gym and look around, mystified. Nothing's there—nothing but parked cars.

And then an enormous roar cuts the air, an ear-splitting *vroom* so loud that you feel it under your fingernails. All attention is wrenched away from the vehicles in the lot to the single car standing in the driveway, revving its enormous engine.

It's an amazing sight. The paint job is bright red with flecks of silver that catch the sunlight and dazzle the eye. Emblazoned on the driver's door is the image of a leaping frog. Sparks fling from the animal's powerful back legs, spraying the full length of the chassis to the rear bumper. There's no hood, and the motor has been raised to full view, shiny and brand-new. Twin tailpipes, gleaming chrome, slash down both sides of the car. Multicolored LED lights flash from every wheel rim.

Stunned and speechless, all I can do is stare. Emma is clamped onto my arm, cutting off the circulation. What does this hot rod have to do with a middle school science fair entry?

The judges are pop-eyed.

"*This* is your project?" the woman from the high school breathes.

The kids nod, tickled pink with themselves.

"It's our working model," Kiana brags.

Aldo leans into the gym and bellows, *"In your face, losers!"*

"They built the engine from parts in my shop," Jake explains, his voice hoarse with pride. "My mechanics supervised, but the kids did all the work."

"They did everything," Emma confirms. "One of them is even the driver."

That's when I recognize Parker at the wheel, grinning so wide that his face is about to break.

"Why is there an elderly woman with him?" the professor wants to know.

"That's Grams," Kiana explains. "It's a long story."

"They did a lot more than just put an engine in," Jake goes on. "You're looking at new tires, rims, glass, wipers, interior. And the body work—remember, this car is twenty-seven years old."

I snap to attention. "Twenty-seven years old?"

I can't believe I didn't see it before. Sure, it's all rebuilt and fancy and souped-up, but the original shape is still there, hidden beneath the tailpipes and the chrome and the blinding paint job.

It's . . . it's . . .

God bless America, it's the Coco Nerd.

# Twenty-Nine
## Parker Elias

I t's worth all the hard work to see Mr. Kermit's face when he recognizes his car, brand-new and so much better. Although how could it be any worse than it was when he left it, being shoveled up off the entrance to the parking lot?

I tap on the gas and listen as the roar echoes off the front of the school building. Some cars purr like a kitten; this one screams like a howler monkey—all thanks to 585 horses under the hood. (If it had a hood.)

*Howler monkey*. I saw that in a book a couple of days ago. At first, it looked like HOLEY WORKMEN, but I figured it out in record time. That's been happening faster and faster lately, thanks to the extra reading help Mr. Kermit has gotten for me.

And not just me. Ribbit helped every kid in our class. There's no way we could ever thank him enough for what he's done, but that doesn't mean we can't try. That's why we rebuilt his car for him. And it's why I have to use this science fair project to totally blow the judges' minds and save his job.

Grams regards the large eggplant in her lap quizzically. "I can't imagine why I bought this pocketbook," she complains. "It doesn't match anything I wear."

"Please don't squeeze it," I request. "It's the blue-plate special at Local Table tonight." If I'm driving, there had better be farm business involved.

At that moment, Kiana raises her arm and drops it. The high sign! I stomp on the gas.

Even I'm shocked by the burst of acceleration as those 585 horses hurl us forward at breakneck speed. In a heartbeat, the others are far behind me in the rearview mirror. The feeling of raw power is so awesome that, when we run out of driveway, I almost forget that I'm the one who's steering the car. At the last instant I yank on the wheel. We thump onto River Street and fly down the block, tires barely touching the pavement. According to Jake, this engine should get us from zero to sixty in 4.6 seconds. By now, we've got to be just about there.

As we pick up speed, Rahim's banner unfurls from the car's old-fashioned radio antenna. I can see it in the mirror, fluttering in the slipstream behind us—the expertly painted words of the message we need to deliver beyond any other:

FIRE RIBBIT? NO WAY!

My classmates are jumping up and down and cheering, so it must be open and readable.

The adults aren't moving at all, which might be from shock. We didn't tell Jake or Miss Fountain about the banner part. And, of course, Mr. Kermit himself didn't suspect any of this until a few seconds ago. (He might not even know he's Ribbit.)

Then everybody's gone as I screech around the corner to circle the block. That's the plan—a quick loop of the school, banner flying, and back up the driveway to stop at the judges' feet so they can examine this monster engine, every inch of it built by us.

By this time, Grams is enjoying the ride. "Where are we going, kiddo?"

"The senior center, like always," I reply, "with a short detour to impress the judges!"

"Judges?" she echoes in a strange tone. "Don't you mean firemen?"

"No, Grams, they're judges," I explain patiently. "This is a science fair project."

She frowns. "Then who's going to put out the fire?"

That's when I spot tongues of bright orange flame in the rearview mirror. I panic. "The car's on fire!"

Grams is totally calm. "No, it isn't, kiddo. It's that rag we're towing."

"The banner!" I risk a glance over my shoulder. She's right! The heat of the tailpipe set fire to the bedsheet fabric we used to make the banner. Come to think of it, Jake mentioned that he filled the gas tank with racing fuel to get maximum performance for the judges. He said it burns really hot! Yeah, no kidding!

What should I do? If I stop, then we won't win the science fair and Mr. Kermit will be gone. But how can I drive a car that's on fire? Well, technically, the car isn't burning—just the sheet attached to the radio antenna. Already, FIRE RIBBIT? NO WAY! is down to FIRE RIBBIT? NO W. It looks like we want him to get fired right now! That's the *opposite* of the message we're trying to send!

I wheel around another corner. Since I can't stop, I speed up, flooring the gas pedal again. Maybe the wind will put out the fire. Instead, it fans the flames. The banner whips from side to side, leaving glowing embers dancing in the air. The next time I look back, a honeysuckle hedge is ablaze. This is definitely not covered under my provisional license!

"Nice moves, kiddo!" Grams cheers. "I never knew you were such a good driver."

All the months I've been driving Grams, and she doesn't notice my skills until I'm laying waste to the neighborhood. As I streak back toward River Street, I leave a line of smoldering bushes in my wake. Black smoke hangs in the air. Now the banner is down to FIRE RIB, which sounds like an ad for a restaurant. All along the sidewalk, people are shouting and pointing and scrambling to get out of the way of the swirling sparks.

Breathing a silent prayer, I make the final turn onto River Street and streak up the school's driveway. Even though this is a disaster, there's only one place to go—back to the judges. Remember, our project isn't Banner Making 101; it's *The Internal Combustion*

*Engine.* And that part works amazing.

Suddenly, some guy in a suit steps from the parking lot right into the road in front of me. I slam on the breaks, sending the car into a skid. At the last second, the suit guy hurls himself out of the way, somersaulting through a flowerbed.

The car fishtails around and lurches to a halt right before the three judges. Mr. Carstairs runs up with a fire extinguisher and puts out the burning banner with a sea of foam. All that's left is a single word, hanging limp from the antenna: FIRE.

Like we didn't already know that.

Half the science fair is out on the lawn, gawking at me in horrified silence. I say the thing I've been rehearsing all along: "Ta-da!"

It doesn't go over as well as I expected.

Jake rushes to help Grams out of the car. The eggplant drops to the pavement and splits open. Miss Fountain comes for me.

From the direction of the flowerbed, the guy I almost hit marches up, red with fury under the layer of mud that cakes his face and expensive suit. Oh man—it's Dr. Thaddeus, the superintendent!

"Who's the driver?" he rages. "I'll have you arrested! You lunatic, how dare you . . ." His voice trails off when he realizes he's talking to a kid.

It's an awkward moment. None of the adults have the guts to say anything, because most of them are teachers, and this mud ball is their boss.

The only person who speaks up is Grams.

"Who do you think you are?" she storms at the stunned Dr. Thaddeus. "You ought to be ashamed of yourself, a lowlife who hasn't got the sense to put on a clean suit! Where do you get off yelling at my grandson—my grandson—"

Then she says it: "—my grandson, Parker!"

Parker.

She called me Parker.

A lot of crazy things happened this morning—like when our banner caught on fire and the eggplant got ruined. And I almost killed the superintendent, obviously.

But for me, today will always be the greatest day ever, because Grams remembered my name.

# Thirty
## Aldo Braff

Just because you've got anger management problems doesn't mean there isn't plenty to be ticked off about.

Second. *The Internal Combustion Engine* finished second in the district science fair. It would have been better to finish 150th than to come *so close* to winning only to take an L. I don't care about the trophy. You can find that plastic junk in any dollar store. But we were a *hair* away from saving Ribbit! And they gave first place to a bunch of dweebs whose teacher didn't even need saving. I barely remember their project—some windmill thingy. No one's ever going to forget ours—definitely not the fire department, who had to spray down all those bushes and trees because of "conflagration containment," whatever that means.

Miss Fountain tries to make us feel better. "You can't take this so personally," she tells us on Monday morning. "Your project was just as good as the wind turbine, but clean power is very hot these days."

"Hot?" I echo. "We set the whole street on fire! What could be hotter than that?"

She's patient. "I mean popular. People care about the environment. Your project was wonderful, but internal combustion engines are so last century."

"How do you think everybody got to the science fair?" Barnstorm challenges. "They drove internal combustion engines."

"I'll bet nobody came by wind turbine," Elaine adds in her usual rumble.

Miss Fountain just sighs. I can't be mad at her. She wanted this every bit as much as we did.

It was Ribbit who showed me that teachers aren't always the enemy, even when they make you do work, or yell, or take away your rabbit butts. If it wasn't for

Ribbit, I never would have heard of *Where the Red Fern Grows*, which I'd be done with by now if we didn't drop everything to work on the science fair. I can barely picture my life before I knew about Billy, Old Dan, and Little Ann, who feel like real people to me—except Old Dan and Little Ann, who are dogs.

"Poor Mr. Kermit," says Kiana. "I can't believe we let him down."

"I don't want any more of that kind of talk," Miss Fountain lectures sternly. "You didn't let him down. Just the opposite—he's prouder of you than he's ever been of any class. And he *loves* his new car."

"Then how come he was afraid to drive it home from the science fair?" Mateo asks.

"That was just because of the racing fuel," she explains. "Once Jake drained all that out and put in regular gas, Mr. Kermit was fine. He has the cutest nickname for it. He calls it Coco Nerd. Isn't that adorable?"

Miss Fountain thinks a lot of things are adorable. That's not my style. Maybe Vladimir, in a lizardy kind of way. And Old Dan and Little Ann, although I never met them in real life.

Anyway, Ribbit might be psyched about his car, but he isn't psyched enough to come to school today.

Even worse, our sub turns out to be Dawn of the Dead again.

To be honest, she's not as mean this time around. Some of that might be that we're so depressed about losing Ribbit that nobody has the energy to give her much of a hard time. We drop a few textbooks, but our hearts aren't into it enough to get the timing right. Who can buzz out a fake power hum when the best teacher in the world is getting shafted—and you could have helped, but you failed? We deserve Dawn of the Dead. We deserve someone even meaner than her. I can't picture who that would be. Mateo probably knows.

When she tells us to work, we don't argue with her. We don't groan and complain. We don't even goof off. I'm just as happy to get back to Old Dan and Little Ann. It might take my mind off Ribbit and how we blew it for him.

Dawn watches us a few minutes. Then she sighs and says, "All right, let's hear it."

We stare at her blankly.

"Come on," she persists. "Something's eating you— all of you. Tell me what it is."

It's like a dam breaks, and we all start jabbering at the same time.

"Our teacher's getting fired for no reason at all!"

"It's not fair!"

"That jerk Thaddeus hates Mr. Kermit!"

"He's worse than the Dementors!"

"I should have run him over when I had the chance!"

It goes on and on. We never run out of complaints about how awful and unfair it is. It's the first time I've ever been in a class where everybody else is just as mad as I am. And we can't *all* have anger management issues.

Sometimes mad is exactly what you're supposed to be.

The amazing part is Dawn of the Dead doesn't chew us out or shut us down. She *listens*, which can't be easy with all seven of us yelling over each other. Then she has a long conversation with Miss Fountain, who comes to see what the racket is about.

The two of them are in the hall talking for what seems like forever. Finally, the substitute walks back into the room and faces us.

"Well, it seems as if I misjudged you young people."

She's wrong about that. Anything bad she thought about us last time goes double. Because we had the opportunity to help Ribbit.

And we came up empty.

# Thirty-One
## Mr. Kermit

The Coco Nerd is back—in a manner of speaking. Not that anybody would recognize it. It bears very little resemblance to the 1992 Chrysler Concorde Fiona picked out all those years ago. It looks like exactly what it is—a mean set of wheels designed by a bunch of eighth graders who think nothing is worth driving unless everybody's staring at it. Chrome. Glitter paint. LED lights. Tailpipes the size of cruise missiles. And an engine you can barely see over.

I'm afraid to honk the horn. I know their taste in music.

Even without the racing fuel, the thing is a rocket. The first time I dare to tap the gas pedal, I nearly rear-end a cement truck. Only Dale Earnhardt Jr. could drive this car. It should be outlawed by the government.

I'm crazy about it. My kids built this for me. It's the second-greatest gift they could have given me—number one being the sight of Superintendent Thaddeus diving headfirst into a muddy flowerbed, coming up fragrant with fertilizer, a chrysanthemum behind his ear.

They're the best class any soon-to-be-ex-teacher could ever hope to have. They even put a frog logo on the door in honor of my last name. Kermit the Frog. Come to think of it, the frog theme has been in place since the beginning of the year—more proof that the so-called Unteachables have better heads on their shoulders than anyone suspected. I just never connected it with all that ribbiting before.

I don't mind. It's kind of a tribute.

On day one, a cop pulls me over just to get a good look at what I'm driving. The officer writes out a ticket giving me one week to cover up the engine.

I call Jake, who promises to design a hood that complies with the law. He also agrees to raise the seat four inches so I'll be able to see the road in front of me.

"I don't want the kids working on it," I insist over the phone. "They've done more than enough for me already."

"I've loved being their sponsor," Jake replies. "They're a fantastic group." A brief pause. "Too bad not all your classes measured up to their level."

He's 1,000 percent right about that. Who'd know better than Jake, who single-handedly made the 1992 class a nightmare and messed up my life in the process?

On the other hand, 1992 was a long time ago. In 1992, the Coco Nerd was just a car. Today it's a weapon of mass destruction. The transformation of Jake Terranova has been no less dramatic. He's a businessman, an entrepreneur. A grown-up. A solid citizen who's done so much for the Unteachables. Plus, a few days ago, I spotted his Porsche parked in front of the Greenwich Diamond Exchange, and Jake himself inside, examining velvet trays of rings.

Fiona's daughter could definitely do worse.

"People change," I tell my former student. "You're—

you're a good guy, Jake."

Jake actually gets choked up on the other end of the line.

I've never ruined anyone's life, but apparently it's almost as hard on the messer as it is on the messee.

I go back to school on Wednesday. Not because I care one way or the other whether the place is still standing, but because I don't want the kids to think I blame them for not winning the science fair. In fact, the opposite is true. They exceeded my wildest expectations. They've been doing that on a daily basis ever since they dumped the vuvuzela shipment in the river.

Another thing about the new and improved Coco Nerd: it's unparkable. Those external tailpipes make it as wide as a ferryboat. But I finally get it jammed in between Emma's Prius and the pickup truck belonging to the Elias farm. The door opens and I have about four inches of clearance to squeeze myself through. Amazingly, I make it. I've been slimming down lately, thanks to the mustard-on-toast diet. Since I'm going to be out of a job soon, maybe it's time to reinvent myself as a weight-loss guru. I'll be rich. Or at least I'll be able to afford gas for the Coco

Nerd's 585-horsepower engine.

I've barely set foot inside the entrance foyer when Principal Vargas rushes up and grabs me by the arm. "Zachary, I need to talk to you."

"Later," I promise her. "I want to reassure my class—"

"Now!" And she literally drags me into her office and shuts the door.

She's obviously been staking out the front hall. It can only mean one thing. Thaddeus is using the events of the science fair to fire me effective immediately. The superintendent is so mad that he won't even let me finish out the semester.

"So," I say bitterly, "is Thaddeus planning to ax me in person, or has he got you doing his dirty work for him?"

In answer, she presses a copy of the *Greenwich Telegraph* into my hands.

I don't even glance down at it. "How do you like it, Christina?" On some level, I regret unloading my emotions on the principal, who has never been anything except supportive. But I'm just too upset to hold it inside. "How does it feel to wield the hatchet for him?"

"Read it, Zachary," she orders.

# SUPERINTENDENT TO SUPER TEACHER: "YOU'RE FIRED!"

The Greenwich Telegraph, Local News
By Martin Landsman, Staff Reporter

It's the goal of every community to create a school system in which each pupil is inspired to excel. This can't be accomplished without great teachers. But an educator who can truly transform the lives of his or her students is the rarest of gems. Meet Mr. Zachary Kermit, teacher of the Self-Contained Special Eighth-Grade Class at Greenwich Middle School. By any objective measure, Mr. Kermit has performed a miracle. His students' test scores are up 87 percent this semester. SCS-8 took second place at the competitive district science fair. Disciplinary problems have virtually disappeared. Most impressive of all, the atmosphere in his classroom—formerly one of Greenwich's most difficult—has become nurturing, supportive, enthusiastic, and successful. And there's no mistaking the students' opinion of their teacher: they adore him.

> And what's Mr. Kermit's reward for this remarkable achievement? A letter of commendation? A bonus? A promotion?
>
> No, a pink slip. He's been terminated, effective the end of the semester. . . .

I read on. The reporter calls out Dr. Thaddeus by name and demands to know why the best teacher in the district is being fired. He accuses the superintendent of holding a personal grudge dating back to the cheating scandal in 1992. And he includes a quote from a member of that 1992 class—prominent local business owner Jake Terranova—guaranteeing that what happened back then wasn't the teacher's fault.

The article concludes:

> Dr. Thaddeus, this message is for you. It's time to put petty grievances aside and remember who our education system is supposed to serve—our children.

I look up at my principal. "Who wrote this?" I squint at the byline. "Who's Martin Landsman, and how did he find out about my class?"

"Beatrice Landsman is the sub who covered your group on Monday. Martin is her son. I guess the kids gave her quite an earful."

"They're something special." I have to work hard to keep my voice steady. "Every time I think I've seen the best they have to offer, they climb one rung higher. That's why I'm anxious to get to my room. We don't have very many more days together."

"That's what I've been trying to tell you!" she exclaims. "Everyone in town has seen this article. The district offices are buried in phone calls and emails. You're not fired anymore!"

I'm stunned. "Thaddeus changed his mind?"

"He didn't have much choice. You're a hero. And that means you can finish out the year and take your early retirement in June. Congratulations, Zachary. I'm so pleased for you."

A flood of relief and satisfaction washes over me. And yet . . . for some reason, I'm not as thrilled as I thought I'd be at such good news. Where's the happy? The joy? The triumph at beating back that overblown, self-important tyrant of a superintendent?

It comes to me in a moment of clarity: the problem isn't the reinstated part. It's the part about retiring in

June. Why would I fight off Thaddeus's attempt to force me out in December only to exit voluntarily a few months later?

The Unteachables have done a lot for me this semester, but their greatest gift is this: they showed me that I'm still a teacher. I have a lot to offer students—not just this class, but many classes to come.

"I'm not retiring," I tell her. "Sign me up for next year."

She stares at me uncertainly. "Zachary?"

I head for the door. "And I want SCS-8. Nobody else. If anyone has questions, I'll be with my kids."

I stride to room 117 with an energy and a sense of purpose I haven't known in decades. By the time I get there, my feet are barely touching the floor. So I'm a little shocked when I see how down the students are. Here I am, on top of the world, and they're positively drooping. Barnstorm's left crutch is the only thing keeping him from falling out of his chair. Rahim's head is on his desk again. But he isn't sleeping; he's just too depressed to sit upright. Even Aldo is missing his usual belligerent expression, making him look almost agreeable. And there isn't a single *ribbit*. Not one.

I sit down on the edge of my desk. "I have an announcement to make."

Kiana stands up. "Us first, Mr. Kermit." Her voice is thin and watery. "We're really sorry we couldn't win the science fair for you. We came so close, but in the end, it just wasn't enough. Maybe it's true what everybody says—that we're a bad class."

I leap to my feet. "Don't ever say that! You're the best class in this school, and I know, because I've been shuffled around to most of them. You've got *nothing* to be sorry for! Besides," I add, realizing I should have said this part first, "I'm not fired anymore."

Heads snap to attention, even Rahim's. Elaine jumps up, sending her chair skittering.

"You're messing with us," Barnstorm accuses.

"For real, Mr. K?" asks Parker, his eyes huge.

"For real," I confirm. "I can't explain it exactly, because I'm not sure I understand it myself. But it has a lot to do with—"

That's as far as I get. They swarm the desk, cheering and howling, almost knocking me over, battering me with high fives. Their behavior is loud, unruly, and borderline violent—completely unacceptable. I accept it. They've earned that much and more.

Emma rushes over from next door to investigate the ruckus.

"Ribbit isn't fired anymore!" Parker yells at her, and

she joins the celebration, unruly as any of the kids.

I can't help noticing that she's wearing an engagement ring—a big one. I'm not her father, but in a strange way, I feel like a proud parent.

"*Enough!* Settle down, everybody!" I glare my Unteachables back to their seats. "Just because we got some good news doesn't mean this isn't a school. Haven't you all got work to do?"

There's a shuffling sound as books, papers, and iPads are pulled out of desks. Aldo and Elaine disappear behind their copies of *Where the Red Fern Grows*.

"That's wonderful, Mr. Kermit," Emma breathes as she heads back to her own class. "We're going to have something inspiring to talk about during Circle Time."

As I sit down, I catch a flash of sunlight reflecting off the red and silver of the Coco Nerd out in the parking lot. We have a lot in common, the car and I. Just like me, it was a beat-up old wreck on the verge of falling apart at any moment. But we were refurbished—both of us—brought back to life by seven Unteachables.

"*No-o-o-o!*"

The cry from Aldo is pure agony.

I turn to him in alarm. "Aldo—what's wrong?"

His face is redder than his hair, and streaked with tears. "Old Dan and Little Ann!" he gasps, waving *Where the Red Fern Grows* in front of him. "They're dead! Both of them!"

"Heavy," Elaine agrees, her expression solemn.

"Well," I begin, choosing my words carefully, "some stories—"

Aldo cuts me off. "I read *one* book all the way through—just one! And this is what I get for it? The cover should come with a sticker: *Warning: Do not read unless you hate dogs!*"

The kid is totally inconsolable. By eighth grade, most readers have already experienced plenty of devastating sad endings. But in Aldo's case, this is the first novel he's ever finished.

I turn to the Goodbunnies chart, pluck a puffy-tail from the Ziploc baggie, and affix it next to Aldo's name.

"Well done. You showed empathy in reacting to a piece of literature. Congratulations."

Aldo seems shocked at first. Then, amid a smattering of applause, he walks to the front of the room, removes his one and only puffy-tail, and offers it to Kiana.

"Fair is fair," he says bravely. "I owe you a lot more than just this one."

"Please keep it," Kiana tells him.

He shakes his head. "It has to work like a market economy."

She looks at me. "Come on, Mr. Kermit. Do I have to take it? Even in a market economy, there's such a thing as giving someone you like a present if you want to."

Aldo's eyes widen, and his hair seems to become just a touch redder—or maybe it's a reflection of the sudden flush in his cheeks.

I issue my ruling. "Absolutely. A lender is allowed to forgive a debt."

And Aldo Braff, the toughest case in the entire Greenwich School District, throws his arms around Kiana and hugs her.

My career has taken some strange detours. Yet here I am, surrounded by the worst class I've ever had in every way but one—the fact that they're the best class I've ever had. Somehow, it feels like I'm exactly where I was meant to be, doing exactly what I was meant to do.

Teaching the Unteachables.

# Thirty-Two

## Kiana Roubini

**M**y mother is going to be a movie star.

Well, not exactly. I guess she's a pretty good actress, though. As soon as her movie wraps in Utah, she gets offered a part in this other film that's shooting next month in British Columbia. This one has a big budget, so it's a great career move. It also means the studio is willing to hire me a tutor so I can go live with Mom while she's on location.

I hope she isn't too upset when I tell her thanks but no thanks.

I actually kind of surprise myself with that answer, considering how anxious I've been to blow this Popsicle stand. And believe me, it's not—repeat, *not*—because Aldo asked me to the Fall Ball, which is this big dance they throw before Thanksgiving break. I'm never going to be the kind of girl who drops everything and changes all her plans because of some guy. Stepmonster did that—she left Chicago to come to Greenwich to marry Dad, and she still regrets it. Not the marrying-Dad part; but she's always complaining that you can't get decent pizza around here.

I know this is pretty unexpected, me being temporary and all. But that's the life of a short-timer. You are one until you aren't anymore. You start putting down roots. I've got friends, and a baby brother who'll be taking his first steps in the next few months. Besides, Stepmonster finally got around to registering me at school, so I probably owe it to her to hang around for a while.

A few days later, Mom calls from the Vancouver airport to see if I've changed my mind. Shooting starts in three more days, so this is the last chance for the studio to bring in a tutor.

"That's okay," I tell her. "I've decided to finish out the year here. Besides," I add, smiling to myself, "you don't hire a tutor for an Unteachable like me."

# More favorites by
# GORDON KORMAN

## THE MASTERMINDS SERIES

BALZER + BRAY
*An Imprint of* HarperCollins*Publishers*

www.harpercollinschildrens.com